CYNTHIA HICKEY

# Troublesome Twosome
(A Tail Waggin' Mystery)
## By Cynthia Hickey

Copyright © **2021 Cynthia Hickey**
**Published by: Winged Publications**

This book is a work of fiction. Names, characters, places, and incidents are the product of the author's imagination and are used fictitiously. Any resemblance to actual events, locales, or persons, living or dead, is coincidental.

No part of this book may be copied or distributed without the author's consent.

All rights reserved.

ISBN: 978-1-952661-64-8

# DEDICATION

To Pet Lovers Everywhere!.

# Chapter One

"It's nice to be back to normal." I smiled as my friends and coworkers fought over who would enter Tail Waggin' first.

"Define normal, Trinity Ashford." Shar glared at Heather. "Respect your elders."

Heather rolled her eyes and stepped back, letting the other woman enter first. "You aren't that old."

After what had happened to us a few weeks ago, I thought the two would stop their squabbling. But, like I said, we were back to normal.

A few minutes after my friends entered, Brad, my boyfriend and the most handsome, sweetest man in the state, carried in four coffees. "Good morning, ladies." He kissed me and handed me my frozen mocha drink.

"Now I can start my day."

"See you after work." Another kiss and he

rushed out the door, no doubt excited that tonight was the grand opening of the finally completed theater.

We'd dated for months, but it wasn't until I emerged victorious after running for my life through the dark woods that we actually said the words, 'I love you' out loud to each other. Since then, things seemed more intimate, more real between us.

"Knock that goofy grin off your face." Shar grinned. "Don't you have some animals arriving soon for boarding?"

"Daycare." I jumped up.

My two cats, Sharkbait and Trashcan, took off like missiles from their seats on the counter, up the stairs to my apartment. Sheba, my one-year-old mastiff, raised her ears and looked at me as if waiting for me to tell her to go after them. I motioned for her to stay and rushed to the back to make sure I had a clean kennel for the dog and cat.

I hadn't taken care of this client's pets before and wanted to make sure everything was perfect so she'd bring her business back. A quick spray of the hose and we were ready for our new guests.

"Why pay for a cat to be at a pet daycare?" Heather shook her head. "If it's just for the day, the cat would be fine at home."

"Maybe it's the woman's—" I glanced at my ledger, "—Mrs. Wells' baby."

David Johnson, our local delivery guy, pushed a dolly piled with boxes into the store. "Ladies." Once upon a time, his dark eyes had landed on me, but now they stayed focused on Heather. I didn't mind. Her divorce from her jailbird, car-stealing husband would be finalized soon, and she'd be free to hang out with a nice guy.

"Put them by the counter." Heather's face reddened, and she ducked her head. "Thank you."

David's smile faded as he stacked the boxes.

"Don't worry," I said, softly. "Ask her out in a month when she's a free woman."

Her husband had been in prison for over six months, so as far as I was concerned, that was long enough for my friend to be alone with her now three-year-old son. They both needed a good man in their lives. Brad had helped with repairs, but my man wasn't there to have meaningful conversations or help with Robbie or whatever husbands helped with.

David's smile returned, teeth flashing against his ebony skin. "I'll do that. Have a good day, ladies."

"If I were only younger." Shar fanned her face with her hand.

"I thought you were after McIlroy?" That's the impression everyone had since we'd met him during our first adventurous mystery.

"That man is as blind as one of those creatures who live deep in a watery cave." She cut viciously into one of the boxes. "Ugh. I cut through a bag of dog food." She stormed out of the front area, returning a few seconds later with a plastic carton and started scooping up kibble.

"Settle down. Our client is here." I hurried to open the door for the woman with one hand holding the leash of a hyper corgi, and the other holding a crate with a very unhappy cat inside.

"Thank you. Honey is a handful and Prince is, well, a diva." Mrs. Wells approached the counter and set the carrier on the floor, the fluorescent lights glittering off the rings on her fingers. "Between the two of them, they can't be trusted not to tear up a place, and I have a hundred and one things to do today. I'll return for them before you close. Oh, and please keep the two of them together. They're inseparable."

She left before I could make that promise. I took the leash and crate, doing my best not to stumble and fall as Honey ran in and around my legs, entangling me. "You little rascal." I did a hop, skip, and jump routine all the way to the kennels.

I eyed the opening at the top. Prince would have no trouble scaling the fence and getting out. "Sorry, you two. It's into the enclosed kennels for you." I chose the largest one and put them both inside, promising to give them exercise time in a bit.

The dog barked, the cat howled, and soon every other daycare pet joined in until the racket made my teeth hurt. Times like this made me grateful I'd taken Sheba to obedience school. Once, she'd been as much trouble as these two.

Shar glanced through the glass window of the grooming station as I passed, eyes wide, hand holding the water sprayer paused over a soaked poodle. I shrugged and continued to the front.

"What in the world is going on back there?" Heather asked.

"Pandemonium." I sat behind the counter and cupped my hands around my head.

"It won't look good for business if someone comes in. When Robbie is riled up, I give him a snack."

"Good idea." I grabbed our best-selling pet treats and returned to the kennels, giving each and every single animal a treat. They all calmed down except for Honey and Prince. No wonder their human wanted them out of her hair for a day.

An hour later, I put the troublesome twosome on leashes and took them to the grassy area we used for exercise. The other animals with us that day were allowed to roam free. These two I didn't trust. Prince hated the leash as evidenced by the twisting, turning, and folding of his body.

"I'm sorry, buddy, but I can't have you getting loose. You'd be like a tiny Godzilla in this town."

I kept checking my watch throughout the day. Hope reared its head every time the bell over the door jingled. Hours passed with no sign of Mrs. Wells.

"If those two were here every day, I'd definitely take my grooming on wheels." Shar referred to the van that had belonged to the deceased Sarah Turner.

"The police released the van to us months ago. Why haven't you?" I glanced up from staring at account ledgers.

"You need me here. Today proves that." She opened the door to the kennels and yelled for Honey to stop barking. It didn't work.

"That was a big help, thanks." I laughed and returned to books that were hard to decipher with so much noise. Maybe I should let the troublesome twosome wander around the store area. I'd try almost anything to get them to settle down.

"Makes you appreciate child daycares, doesn't it?" Heather shuddered.

I decided to leave the two in their kennels.

When five o'clock rolled around with no sign of Mrs. Wells, I called her. No answer. I sent Shar and Heather home and hung around until Brad showed up at five-thirty.

"What do you want to do?" He asked, grimacing at the noise coming from the cat carrier. "That dog is going to hang itself if she doesn't sit."

Sure enough, Honey had tangled herself around the playpen. "We could drive to Mrs. Wells' house and drop them off."

"All right, but let's take your car. Sheba is fine to ride in the Mercedes but not that little scamp."

"Sheba will stay here." I took her upstairs to the apartment, fed her and the cats, then rejoined Brad. "I feel terrible about this, but I'm going to let Mrs. Wells know that I can't watch her pets again. Not until they learn to behave at least a little bit."

"Don't feel bad. I don't know how you made it through the day." He picked up the dog, leaving me to take the cat. Honey settled right down. "I guess she just wants to be held."

I sighed and locked the door behind us. Maybe I could find someone to cuddle the animals like volunteers do at a hospital nursery.

I set the carrier in the backseat and, since Honey liked Brad, left her to him and climbed into the driver's seat. "She doesn't live far." I put the address I'd memorized into the GPS. Ritzy area.

Fifteen minutes later, I drove around one of the

largest fountains I'd ever seen in someone's yard and parked in front of a plantation-style house flanked by magnolia trees. I'd always envisioned myself someday living in such a place or in one of those country homes with a wraparound porch. Maybe I'd decide by the time I got married.

I followed Brad to the porch. He stopped so suddenly I ran into him, smashing my nose on his back. "What's wrong?"

"The door is open."

I peered around him to see the door ajar a couple of inches. "Mrs. Wells?" When no answer came, I pushed the door open further. "Hello?"

Brad put Honey down. "Lead the way, girl."

The dog wagged her tail and turned left, leading us to the kitchen and her food dish. A one-track mind, this one. I turned around and headed for the sweeping staircase. "Mrs. Wells?" The hair on my arms stood at attention. I'd had the same reaction when I'd found Brad's father murdered in his bed.

Hoping I overreacted, I climbed the stairs with heavier footsteps than normal so I didn't startle the woman if she was home. I opened two carved double doors and stepped into a ransacked room. Armoire doors hung open. Blankets were wadded on the thick carpeted floor. I headed for the door on my left. An empty jewelry box mocked me from the dresser.

I swallowed past the dryness in my throat and entered the bathroom. "Brad?"

Mrs. Wells lay on the marble floor, a silk scarf around her neck. I reached under the scarf, feeling a fine gold chain tangled in the fabric and felt for a pulse. The chill of her skin answered the question. "I found her. Guess what? She's Dead."

# Chapter Two

"You couldn't make it through the summer, could you?" Detective McIlroy stared at Mrs. Wells' body but spoke to me.

"It wasn't my fault." I crossed my arms and glared. "I can't help it if I have a tendency to find dead bodies. It looks like a robbery gone wrong."

"Thank you, Miss Sherlock, but I know how to do my job. Officer Rickson, please contain the scene."

Waterfall's newest officer nodded and left the room—I assumed he went to get the yellow crime scene tape I'd become very familiar with.

"Because of you, Trinity, we've hired another officer. Meet a veteran in law enforcement, Officer Prentiss."

I turned and met the cold stare of a well-built man in his fifties. Chances were, the two of us would not be friends.

"I've read the articles on Miss Ashford," he said. "Seems to me she enjoys the limelight."

"Are you insinuating I killed someone for the attention?" My mouth dropped open. How could McIlroy have hired someone so stupid?

He shrugged. "Seems suspicious to me."

Of all the thick-headed, addle-brained… "I'm ready to leave, Brad." Head high, I stormed to the door.

"Please do not leave the animals," McIlroy said.

"I don't want them. My apartment is too small."

"I'll take Honey," Brad offered. "I doubt Moses will enjoy Prince, but until other arrangements can be made, I'll take him, too." He scooped the cat off the top of the armoire, fought to stuff it into its carrier, and then called the dog who was hiding in the bathroom.

Outside, Brad stopped next to the car and touched my cheek. "Don't take it personal, sweetheart. The man doesn't know you. He'll come around."

"He thinks I killed Mrs. Wells for the publicity."

"But you didn't." He put Honey and the cat carrier in the backseat. "Let's go home. We have a grand opening to attend."

That's right, and I'd purchased a brand new dress, the color of milk chocolate. Not a used dress from Someone Else's Junk as I normally did, but this time I splurged on something new. I knew how much this theater meant to Brad and wanted everything to be perfect for him. "Are you sure about these two?" I jerked my thumb toward the animals in the back. "They're a lot of work, and that's being nice."

He laughed. "Honey seems to like me. Not sure

about the cat, but we'll see. If we keep this up, we'll have to buy a farm."

"We can't keep every pet left behind when someone dies." I slid into the driver's seat.

"I have a great idea." He clicked his seatbelt into place. "Why not foster these types of animals? You know, the ones left behind until someone adopts them? It would put a few more dollars in your pocket."

I cut him a sideways glance. "You're always thinking of ways to make money."

"My dad and I didn't acquire our wealth by chance. We worked for it. It wouldn't be any different than selling puppies. Just post their photos and wait. Someone will want them."

Glancing in the rearview mirror to where Honey sat, I said, "As long as there's no return policy."

I dropped Brad off at his high-scale apartment complex, then drove home to get ready. Since I lived above my store, which was across the parking lot from the new theater, I'd agreed to meet Brad there at eight.

As I showered, I couldn't erase the picture of Mrs. Wells from my head. Could it really have been a robber she surprised and was killed as a result? Since the past months had been filled with the evils of corrupt businessmen, I had a hard time believing her death could be that simple.

Maybe I'd become jaded over the last few months of helping local law enforcement solve a couple of murders. I really wanted to stay out of things this time, but if Prentiss continued with his insane idea that I killed Mrs. Wells, I'd have to clear my name, right?

Tonight wasn't the time to dwell on such things. I had a party to attend with the state's most eligible bachelor. I dried my hair, letting the curls bounce around my shoulders, put on enough makeup to highlight my best features, then slipped into the sheath dress, adding a gold chain with a dangling pearl. There. I smiled in the mirror. I should look fine next to Brad.

I met up with Shar as I crossed the parking lot. My eyes widened at the bright yellow sequined dress she wore. It looked more fitting for a high school prom than a grand opening.

"Do you think McIlroy will notice me?" She smoothed her hands down the skirt.

"Oh, I doubt anyone can miss you." I stifled a grin.

"It wouldn't hurt you to add some vibrancy to your wardrobe. Black, brown, maroon…"

"You have your style, I have mine." Thank goodness. As we approached the theater, I told her about finding Mrs. Wells. "The new officer actually hinted that I killed her for attention."

"He isn't very bright then, is he?" Her bright red lips curled into a smile. "There's McIlroy. The other man must be the new guy."

"They're here for security." Right along with the local newspaper. The *Waterfall Gazette*'s reporter, Lindsey Grimes, and photographer, Donald Placen, were there. Donald snapped a photo of me and Shar as we stepped onto the red carpet.

I glanced at Officer Prentiss in time to see his lip curl. I stuck my nose in the air and entered the theater. Inside, the aroma of popcorn and butter greeted me. Teenagers lined up behind the concession stand. To my right, a bar beckoned adults to grab a drink and relax. To my left, video games attracted the attention of the younger crowd. Brad had thought of everything.

Posters of now playing movies and new releases adorned the walls. A crystal chandelier hung from the ceiling, showcasing oil paintings of famous actors and actresses from Hollywood's golden age. Once he'd started the decoration process, he hadn't let me inside. It was a far cry from how it looked when Brad and I were almost killed here.

"Like it?" Brad's arms snaked around my waist as cameras flashed.

"It's absolutely beautiful. Too grand for this town, that's for sure, but people will flock here from other towns because of the ambiance."

"That's what I'm hoping." He waved to a man in a suit across the way. "You hungry?"

"I'd love some of that popcorn." Nothing in the world like movie popcorn.

Brad led me to a red velvet chair with promises to return with my refreshment. When he'd left, Lindsey Grimes sat next to me.

"Heard you found Mrs. Wells."

"News travels fast."

"It's my job to know what's going on." She shrugged. "Mind telling me about it for the paper?"

I glanced up and met Prentiss's gaze again. "I'd better not. It's an ongoing investigation."

"I may be new to town, but I've heard that never stopped you before. If you change your mind, I'd love an exclusive." She moved on to someone else, leaving me to squirm under the scrutiny of Officer Prentiss.

Shar joined me. "He sure is burning a hole in you."

"The reporter was here. I'm sure it added to his 'crazy' theory." I smiled up as Brad handed me a diet soda and a bag of popcorn.

"I have to mingle. Will you be all right, or would you like to come with me?"

"I'll catch up to you later." I wasn't the best at conversing with strangers. "I promise."

"Good. I want to show you off." He winked and strolled away, looking very fine in his tailored suit.

"What's our plan?" Shar accepted a flute of champagne from a passing waiter in a red jacket.

"Regarding?"

"Don't be coy. You know you want to dig into this recent murder." She raised the flute to her lips, her gaze on McIlroy. "Do you think he'd be jealous if I went after the stone-faced Prentiss?"

"I don't know, and I don't want to get involved this time. It doesn't concern me." I popped a piece of popcorn in my mouth, reveling in the smooth butter and parmesan coating.

"It does if Prentiss convinces people that you're the culprit."

I sighed. "I don't see how anyone would believe him, least of all McIlroy. He's the one who started all this when he asked for help with the murder of Brad's father. I was content to complain about the lack of funds I needed for veterinary school."

My dreams had changed since then. With the

addition of a groomer and selling pets on consignment, my job was busy and my bank account growing. All because Brad had pushed me to become a better businesswoman.

"I'm going to find Brad. I can't stand that man staring at me anymore." I got up, taking my popcorn and drink with me, and went off in search of my boyfriend.

Spotting him leaning against a second concession stand down the hallway leading to the theaters, I froze. A woman caressed his arm. Brad smiled down at her. When he saw me, he smiled and came my way.

"Who's that?" I glanced up at him, every insecurity I'd fought to keep at bay rising up. The tall, willowy blonde definitely looked better at his side than I ever could.

"Let me introduce you." He put his hand on the small of my back. "This is Vivian Rhodes. We were business partners before I settled in Waterfall. Vivian, this is my girlfriend, Trinity Ashford. She owns the pet daycare Tail Waggin'."

The woman's smile didn't quite reach her blue eyes. "I see now why Brad didn't come home. You're as charming as this quaint little town."

Somehow, she made charming and quaint not sound derogatory. "Pleased to meet you."

"Oh, she even has a sweet accent." Vivian chuckled. "You're the cutest, but I must be going. Lots of networking to be done. Please call me for dinner while I'm here, Brad." Her fingers trailed across his shoulders as she sashayed away, hips slightly swinging in her figure-hugging dress.

"Ex-partner or ex-girlfriend?" I gasped, not meaning to voice my thought.

"Jealous?" Brad pulled me into a dark theater. "You have nothing to worry about, sweetheart." He set the popcorn and soda on a chair. "Let me show you how little she means to me."

I swore my heart would beat free of my chest as he pulled me close and claimed my lips. He kissed me until I couldn't breathe. I leaned into him, relishing the feel of being in his arms.

"Convinced?" His breath ruffled my hair.

"It might take a bit more convincing."

His chest rumbled under my cheek. "I'll enjoy proving it to you. Come. I've a party to attend." He took my hand in his and led me back to the main room.

I stayed close by his side while still engaging in one of my favorite pastimes—people watching.

A young man slipped from behind the concession counter and hurried down the hall making me realize I'd left my popcorn and soda in the clean theater. "I'll be right back."

I followed the young man. "Excuse me." Maybe he wouldn't mind fetching my trash.

He glanced back, then increased his speed, passing the theater Brad had led me into. The young man disappeared around a corner.

Strange behavior from a server. I ducked into the theater and retrieved my things, dropping them in a trashcan. As I exited theater number one, loud voices came from the direction the young man had gone.

I stood there torn between going to investigate

and finding Brad. A gunshot rang out making the decision for me. I made a mad dash to the party, careening into Officer Prentiss who sprinted in my direction.

The suspicious look in his eyes didn't bode well for me. I pointed in the direction the young man had run, then followed Prentiss, McIlroy, and Brad as they raced that way.

They entered theater number ten. "Keep everyone out," McIlroy ordered.

I snuck a peek around him. The young man in a red jacket stared sightless at the ceiling, a bullet hole between his eyes.

"Body count is rising faster this time," Shar said behind me.

# Chapter Three

"Does anyone else think it strange that Miss Ashford always seems to be where a murdered victim is?" Prentiss asked.

Everyone said no at the same time.

"It's a curse," Shar said.

"A talent for trouble," McIlroy added, "but she has a good head on her shoulders."

"A nose for attention is more like it." The officer curled his lip.

"I don't think you've been in town long enough to form those conclusions." Brad put his arm around my shoulders. "If not for Trinity, there'd be two fewer killers behind bars."

"Still seems fishy that it's always her. Aren't there other smart people in this city?" He arched a brow.

I refused to let him bother me. Instead, I slipped from the theater to wait until I had to give my statement. I stifled a frown as Vivian slipped past

Officer Rickson, who I assumed had the task of crowd control. Right on her heels were the reporter and photographer.

Once again I found Donald snapping my photo. Lindsey thrust her microphone in my face while Vivian squeezed past me into the theater.

"Can you tell us what happened?" Lindsey asked. "Was someone shot? Were they killed?"

"No comment." I crossed my arms and looked as stern as I could. Which probably failed. I couldn't get the idea that Prentiss might be a problem out of my head. It became more and more apparent I needed to find out what was going on in order to prove him wrong. The problem, though…he'd be watching my every move.

"Please come back inside so I can take your statement."

I grimaced at Prentiss's request. Taking a deep breath, I stepped back into the dim room.

"I hope you weren't talking to the reporters."

"I wasn't." I lowered to a plush theater seat wanting to tell him I wasn't an idiot but also not wanting to speak to him at all. Since I knew the drill, I spilled the night's events. "I saw this guy slip away from the concession stand. He acted suspicious so I followed him. He ducked around the corner. I heard loud voices. While I was trying to decide whether to investigate, a gunshot rang out. I ran back toward the main area of the theater and met up with y'all. That's it."

"Do you always follow suspicious people?"

"If my instincts say to."

"You aren't a law enforcement officer, Miss

Ashford. Why investigate?"

"I'm naturally nosy."

"Did you catch a glimpse of the shooter?"

"No. My guess is he ran out one of the exits." I pointed to an exit on each side of the big screen.

He made a noise in his throat. "Since you're such an expert, you know not to leave town."

"Yep." I removed my heels and leaned back in the seats which happened to recline.

Poor Brad. Opening night marred by death. Of course, whatever movie played in number ten would sell out just so the town's teens could say they were in a place where a murder occurred.

I glanced to where Brad and Vivian conversed quietly in a dark corner. Why the long conversation if they were ex-business partners? I squelched the spark of jealousy. Either I could trust my man or we didn't have a relationship after all.

The party had broken up and the guests gone, except for the reporter and her photographer, by the time McIlroy told us we could go. Lindsey fired questions after us as we headed out the double glass doors, clearly frustrated that we were ignoring her.

Outside, I spun toward McIlroy. "I'd rather talk to you if there are more questions regarding my involvement. Officer Prentiss and I don't seem to get along."

He exhaled sharply. "Sorry, but I'm taking a very much needed vacation. Officer Prentiss will be handling this investigation. If things get too bad, I'll cut my vacation short. Try to stay out of his hair, and you'll be fine."

Code for stay out of this one. "He thinks I'm the

killer."

McIlroy chuckled. "He's searching for your gun in the theater, thinking you've stashed it somewhere."

"By focusing on me, he's not trying to find the real murderer. This boy's death and Mrs. Wells' murder might not be related."

"True. Prentiss is a good cop. He'll figure it out. Goodnight." He marched to his car, a spring in his step, no doubt vacation in his mind.

"I'm going to miss him," Shar said.

"Go after Prentiss. Keep him away from me."

She shuddered. "The man's like a block of ice. What's our next move?"

"Find out whether these two murders are related."

The next morning I opened Tail Waggin', my eyes gritty from lack of sleep—something that had become all too familiar. I smiled as Brad strolled down the sidewalk toward me, coffee in one hand, cat carrier in the other, and Honey's leash draped around his wrist.

"Figured you needed this right away as much as I do." He placed a kiss on my neck that sent shivers through me.

"You're the best. Do you have a few minutes?"

"A few." He followed me inside to the small table in the corner, then let the pets run free.

"Sorry about the grand opening."

"Can't beat the promotion, though. People are buying advance movie tickets in droves." He sighed. "Why does it take a murder to bring people in?"

I shrugged. "How did the troublesome twosome do last night?"

"I've cat scratches in the back of my sofa, and Honey chewed up a throw pillow while I was gone. Once I returned home, the two settled right down. Moses watched the whole thing in disdain, I'm sure." He took a sip of his coffee. "I'm not keeping them, so please put that advertisement up asap. My penthouse and my sanity won't survive."

"Too bad we can't put them to work solving crimes like my Sheba." I reached down and petted my baby on her massive head. "But, I doubt even she can help this time."

The bell over the door jingled. Since we weren't open for business yet, I expected Heather or Shar. Instead, a well-dressed woman in a business suit entered.

"Are you the lady who found my mother's body?" She strode to the table, her heels clicking on the tiled floor.

"If your mother was Mrs. Wells, then yes." I stood and offered my hand. "I'm Trinity Ashford. Sorry for your loss."

She returned the shake. "Valerie Smythe. "We weren't close. Would you be willing to meet me at my mother's place? I want you to walk me through what you saw. There are some valuable pieces of jewelry missing, and I've heard you're the one to help me find them."

I stared wide-eyed at Brad, then back at her. "Who told you that?"

"This morning's paper." She pulled a rolled newspaper from her briefcase and set it on the table.

I glanced at the front page and read, "Local Mystery Solver Knee Deep in Another One." I'd wring Lindsey's neck. This would not help with Prentiss at all. "I'm a store owner not a detective."

"I'll pay you five-thousand dollars per item you find."

Well, that was tempting. "I can meet you in an hour after my employees arrive."

"Perfect." She gave a thin-lipped smile. "Is that my mother's dog?"

"Yes, I'm sure you'll want to take her pets."

"Not on your life." With a toss of her head, she marched from the store.

I'd take the animals with me when I met up with her. Maybe I could convince her to change her mind. "What are your plans for today?" I turned back to Brad.

"Some phone meetings. I'll be finished by the time you get off work. How does Chinese sound?"

"Perfect."

When Heather and Shar arrived, I quickly filled them in on Valerie and promised to return as soon as possible. Both were relieved when I gathered up Honey and Prince. The cat had already knocked over a display of dog clothes and the corgi chewed the corner of the counter.

I put them in the backseat of my SUV, donned some headphones so I could drown out their howls with music, and drove to meet Valerie. She stood on the street side of the crime scene tape.

"I thought this would be down by now." She frowned at the sight of the animals. "I don't want them."

"I can't keep them." I smiled. "Don't worry about the tape. I have an in with the detective." I released Honey who darted for the front door.

Valerie pulled a keyring from her purse and unlocked the door. She stepped inside and gasped. "Must thieves destroy things? Why not look and take without destruction?"

"No morals, I guess." Since crime scene tape had blocked the porch, no one had access. The place was exactly as it was when I'd found Mrs. Wells. "You think your mother had hiding places the thief wouldn't know to look in?"

"My mother was a cautious woman." She headed up the stairs toward the master bedroom.

"Hold on. Don't go in until I say." I rushed into the room, grabbed a towel from the bathroom, and spread it across the bloodstain on the floor. "Okay."

Valerie paled at the sight of the towel. "Thank you. That was thoughtful." She knelt at the end of the bed and removed a panel that looked like part of the carved wood. Then she pulled out a black silk bag. "Her pearls."

"Clever." I took the bag she tossed to me.

Not finding anything else, she turned in a slow circle, her gaze scanning the room. "Ah." She removed a framed portrait of a little blonde girl from the wall. Taped to the back was a gold chain.

"You were a cutie."

"This isn't me. That's why I suspected another of mother's hiding places."

"It must have taken her forever to get ready in the mornings." I took the necklace. As the search continued, and the items in my hands grew in number, I couldn't help but wonder why, exactly, she asked me to come along.

Honey sat at my feet, tail wagging, clearly interested in the proceedings. I wondered... Removing her collar, I ran my hands down the pink rhinestones and felt a clasp on the underside. I pressed it and pulled out a tennis bracelet. It would take forever to find all her jewelry at this rate.

Valerie clapped. "Five thousand dollars for you. I was wondering when you'd actually start searching."

That's all the encouragement I needed. I placed the jewelry on the dresser and continued using my imagination to find the missing items. My admiration for Valerie's mother grew. I'd thought Sarah Turner, a woman whose killer I'd helped catch, had been clever to hide a Jumpdrive in an empty dog shampoo bottle. Mrs. Wells put her to shame.

I found a ruby ring in a fake bar of soap in the shower caddy. An emerald ring in a box of half-eaten chocolates. The longer we searched, the more frantic Valerie became, and the richer I did— twenty-thousand dollars of items to be credited to me. I'd never had so much fun in my life.

"It's not here. Mother never hid her jewelry anywhere but in her bedroom and bathroom. Said she didn't like traipsing all over the house for her things."

"What's missing?"

"A diamond necklace and a tiara that are worth a hundred thousand together."

"Where could your mother have possibly hid

them where a stranger could find them?"

"That's what I'm hiring you to find out. Consider the twenty thousand partial payment. I'll double that if you find the missing pieces. It has to be someone she knew and trusted."

# Chapter Four

Wow. A rare moment of speechlessness came over me. I wasn't a detective. I was a pet daycare owner. But I did seem to have a talent for tracking a trail of clues, and we were talking serious money here. This time I only had one clue…that the thief had to be someone Mrs. Wells trusted.

"Of course, it would be you."

I whirled to meet the stern stare of Prentiss. "This is Mrs. Wells' daughter, Valerie Smythe."

He barely spared the woman a glance. "It's a crime to enter a crime scene. What are the two of you doing here?"

"Taking inventory." She motioned to the pile of jewels on the bed. "Only two items are missing. A diamond necklace and a tiara. I suspect the culprit is someone my mother trusted." She crossed her arms. "It seems Miss Ashford and I have already found out more than the local police department."

A muscle ticked in his square jaw. "Detective

McIlroy may think you're an asset, Miss Ashford, but I assure you I don't share the same thoughts. Interfere in my investigation and I will arrest you."

Valerie stood toe-to-toe with him. "I assure *you*, Officer, that Miss Ashford is simply helping me find what is rightfully mine. You cannot stop us from doing that."

His eyes narrowed. "Don't doubt what I can or cannot do. You don't seem to be grieving very much, Ms. Smythe." He whirled and stormed from the room.

I never thought I'd say that I missed McIlroy, but I did. Very much. "I'll need a list of everyone your mother knew in Waterfall."

"All I can give you is the contact list from her phone. I'll bring it to you as soon as I have the names and numbers written down." She smiled. "Don't worry about that old badger. I have it on good authority he's being watched for not doing a good job at his prior location and is out to prove the naysayers wrong."

That was worse than him simply being a jerk. He felt he had something to prove. If he arrested me, folks might look differently at me and my business. If that happened, the money I'd just earned wouldn't last long.

"I can't take the animals," she said. "I'm staying in a ritzy hotel and they don't allow pets. Back home, it's the same. I'll get you that list." She smiled and left me to retrieve her mother's pets.

"What am I going to do with the two of you?" I slid Prince into his carrier. How horrible to be unwanted. Hopefully, the ad I'd placed would find them a forever home.

I headed to my apartment to wait for Brad to bring dinner. Trashcan and Sharkbait were not happy about a stuck-up feline in their midst and hissed when Prince strolled by, tail in the air. The dogs fared a little better, both still closer to being puppies than full-grown.

Five animals in my tiny apartment, one of them a growing mastiff, left me feeling claustrophobic. I carried Honey and Prince to the kennels, putting the unhappy cat in one of the enclosed cages and Honey in one where she could move around a little. "Sorry, you two. Way too crowded upstairs."

My gaze fell on the rhinestone collar Prince wore. I knew it wasn't large enough to hide even a bracelet as Honey's had, but maybe…

I removed the collar and felt the leather on the back. Ah ha. A bump that shouldn't be there. A few minutes later, I held a small key in the palm of my hand.

"What are you doing in here?" Brad joined me.

"Putting these two where they can't cause problems. Do you know what this might go to?"

"A small safe? Safety deposit box, maybe." He tucked a strand of hair behind my ear. "Come eat and tell me what you've been up to."

While we ate, his hand paused on its way to his mouth several times as I told him about my evening. When I finished, he wiped his mouth, then leaned his elbows on the table. "She paid you $20,000 for helping her find hidden jewelry?"

"Yep." I grinned. "Easiest money ever. She'll give me another twenty if I find the necklace and tiara."

"McIlroy is right. Maybe you should apply for a private investigator license." He straightened. "At least then you'd get paid for people trying to kill you."

"I already have a job." I dug into a box of fried rice. From the look on his face, I could tell it took all his will power not to overstep the boundary I'd placed regarding my independence. "Valerie's mother was brutally murdered, and she's asked for my help. I couldn't say no."

"Yes, you could. You put your tongue against the back of your teeth and make the sound. The police are handling this."

"Right. The very police who think I'm making all this up for attention." I tossed down my fork. "Prentiss can't focus his mind on solving this case because he's blinded by being an idiot."

"He's trying to make a fresh start in a new town." Brad crossed his arms.

"He's trying to prove something. Valerie said it herself."

"How do you know you can trust a woman you just met who only seems concerned about her mother's wealth instead of the fact she was murdered?"

Good point. I had to agree with Prentiss that Valerie did not seem to be grieving. What if she killed her mother for the jewelry? She knew where everything was hidden. Valerie could have killed Mrs. Wells because she wouldn't say where the missing items were.

I drummed my fingers on the table. But then,

she wouldn't be giving me a list of contacts. Nor would she have hired me to help her. "She might not be as sad as we all think she should be, but she is entitled to the stolen items."

"Granted, but do you have to be the one?" He sighed. "Are we having our first real fight?"

"Are we?" I tilted my head. "This is me, Brad. Nosy, stubborn, loves animals, tends to find trouble…can you deal with it?"

He stood and pulled me from my chair into his arms. "I'll have to, won't I?" His hands slid through my hair, cradling my head. "To walk away would destroy me." He lowered his head, claimed my lips, and took me to heaven.

A smile still graced my lips the next morning as I jumped out of bed. I showered, dressed, and called for my fur babies to follow me downstairs. I had animals to feed. Once Valerie brought me the list, I'd have some digging into backgrounds to do.

I couldn't wait to tell my friends who listened with wide eyes as Brad had the night before. "Can you believe it? Taking in Honey and Prince has led to a nice chunk of change."

"Seriously?" Shar shook her head. "You have all the luck. I have helped you with every single murder case."

"I hope you will with this one, too." In order to soothe her ruffled feathers, I offered to pay her half of what we received for finding the necklace and the tiara.

"What happens if you don't?" Heather asked. "What if the killer comes for you?"

"Why would he or she? I don't know anything.

All I'm doing is looking for stolen items."

She shook her head. "That's what you always say, and look what happens. Someone comes after you."

I shrugged. "I'll be careful."

"Again, that's what you always say." She marched to the storeroom.

"Ignore her. She's got a burr in her bobby sock," Shar said. "Her divorce is final today. She had to go to the courthouse on her lunch hour."

Why hadn't she told me? I hurried after her. "You can take the day off if you need to."

"Working keeps me sane." She sagged against a stack of dog food bags, tears filling her eyes. "I'll be a divorced woman whose imprisoned husband can't pay child support, yet I have to pay the bills he racked up before going to prison. It's not fair."

"I'm sorry. I wish there was something I could do."

"Just keep this business running so I have a job." She gave a faint smile. "If I hadn't had to run for my life a couple of months ago, I'd offer to help you look for the jewelry. That was too close for comfort. I'll stay right here."

"Let me know if you want to leave." I hugged her. "Don't hurry back or worry if the court thing takes longer than you thought. We can handle things here." After all, I'd left her holding down the store plenty of times.

"Thank you." She sniffed and dried her eyes on a napkin.

I returned to the front in time to see Valerie striding across the parking lot. I opened the door for her.

"Here it is." She waved a sheet of paper. "The killer is bound to be in town somewhere. Call me if you find out anything." Valerie turned to go.

"Wait." I fished the key I'd found from my pocket. "This was in the cat's collar. Know what it goes to?"

She shrugged. "Haven't a clue. My mother doesn't have a safe that I know of. I'll contact the bank. If she had a safety deposit box, I'll tell them to allow you to look inside. I have to go away for a few days. I'll check back in with you when I return. My phone number is on that list. Good luck."

I'd need it. Paper in hand, I sat in my office chair behind the counter. I knew most of the names. Mr. Mills who owned the hardware store, Millie Hedford of Style Yourself, Mrs. Parker who owned the drugstore, Mrs. Murdock of my favorite thrift store…everyone who had a shop in the U-shaped strip mall was here. I couldn't imagine any of them being a killer.

There were a few names I didn't recognize. I'd start there, taking notes on whatever I could find about each person.

The bell over the door jingled, catching my attention. A well-dressed woman around sixty-years-old entered. Her silver hair bobbed around her shoulders, drawing my attention to a beautiful pearl necklace.

"Hello. I'm Irma Grable. Alice Wells and I were dear friends. I saw your post about her pets and would like to take them off your hands."

"That would be wonderful." I jumped up from

my chair. "I'll get them for you right now, although I must warn you they are a handful."

"I know." She smiled. "But Alice would have liked for me to keep them."

I was more than happy to be rid of the furry, troublemaking duo. So happy in fact, that I gave Mrs. Grable enough food for each animal to last a few weeks. "No charge," I said when she opened her wallet. "I'm glad they're going to a friend."

"If you're sure." She wrapped Honey's leash around her wrist and picked up the carrier. "I live in Blytheville, just down from Alice's home. They'll have plenty of room to roam."

I settled back in my chair as she left, relieved that the two cuties were gone, and turned my attention back to my laptop. Time to start digging into people's backgrounds. Not an easy task to do without hacking skills, I soon discovered.

Groaning, I tapped a pencil on my desk. "This is impossible."

"What is?" Shar came around the corner.

"Looking up information on people. Unless they've been in the news, I can't find anything."

"I know someone." She wiggled her eyebrows. "An old boyfriend who is quite savvy on the computer."

"Will he help?"

"Of course. All I'll have to do is ask, maybe go to dinner. We parted on good terms." She pulled her cell phone from her purse. "Circle the names you want him to check."

"I want him to check them all."

Her brows rose. "Some of those are our

friends."

"Even friends have been known to kill for what they think is the right reason."

# Chapter Five

A long three days later with me feeling as if I was wasting Valerie's money, Shar slapped a stack of papers on my desk. "This town is full of secrets."

"Worse than the men having a lady on the side who exchanges gossip at the club on Ladies Night?" It would take me forever to go through all these pages.

"Oh, yes." She tapped the stack. "And that Irma Grable used to be quite the loosey-goosey lady back in her day. You might want to rethink giving her Mrs. Wells' animals."

I shrugged. Someone's past didn't necessarily make them a bad pet owner. "Your guy friend must have dug deep to get all this." I'd focus on a reason to steal jewels and disregard the rest. It would still be a massive project.

"Want me to come over later and go through them with you?"

"That would be a big help." I'd ask Brad, too. With the three of us, it shouldn't be too bad. Plus, I could go through some while at work. We didn't have any new puppies or kittens to sell. Other than the pets being dropped off for daycare and the occasional shopper, I'd have some time.

The first page featured our very own hardware store owner, Mr. Mills. I scanned the page, excitement growing as I read how he'd spent time in jail for unpaid parking tickets. I drummed my fingers on the counter. Not really a reason to kill unless he needed money.

"What if it wasn't about the money?"

Shar's brow furrowed. "What do you mean? It's always about the money."

"We're assuming, based on Valerie's say-so. Mrs. Wells was killed but nothing taken." I held up a hand to stop her protest. "I know the place was ransacked, and we suspect she knew the person, but what if her murder was more personal?"

"Like you said, this town is full of secrets. Maybe she stumbled across a juicy one. If the thief, assuming it is a thief, wanted to steal, she had other jewelry not as fine but still nice, not to mention electronics. Why not take the jewelry she was wearing?" She'd been wearing a gold chain, and while I hadn't dwelled on the fact, I now remembered her rings. Rings that Valerie hadn't needed to search for.

Shar leaned on the counter. "You might be on to something. When you go through those papers, you need to focus on not only a reason to steal but a reason to kill."

Nodding, I turned back to the papers, feeling a bit guilty about digging through other people's dirty linen. I took a legal-size notepad from a drawer. At the top of the pages I wrote People with Reasons to Kill Mrs. Wells. Then, I started rewriting the contact list on my pad, leaving room for notes. I could take care of questioning my fellow mall renters easily enough by visiting them.

I'd bring up the subject of Mrs. Wells' death and let the conversation carry on from there. One could learn a lot from body language and tone of voice.

When Heather arrived, a little late because of a toddler's tantrum about having to wear pants to daycare, I headed down the sidewalk, notepad in a carry bag, and entered the hardware store.

"Good morning, Mr. Mills. I need some lightbulbs." I smiled and leaned on the counter.

Never one to pass out free smiles, he nodded and moved to a metal shelving unit. "Pack of four?"

"Yes. Sad about Mrs. Wells, isn't it? You have heard of her murder, right?"

He set a package of fluorescent lights on the counter. "Of course, I have. A person would have to be an idiot or hiding in a cave not to know one of the town's prominent citizens was brutally killed."

"She lived in Blytheville."

"Close enough to be counted as part of this town."

"Were you friends? Her daughter said you were in her contact list."

"Because she purchased a lot of things from me. She was nice enough." He narrowed his eyes. "You're snooping again, aren't you?"

"Simply making conversation. Please have these

lights delivered. I have other calls to make."

"Curiosity killed the cat, Miss Ashford." His warning followed me out the door.

I quickly jotted down snippets of our conversation, then continued to the salon. The odor of perms and nail polish assaulted my senses the second I opened the door. Only two of the four stylists were busy with customers, not counting the nail technician.

"Trinity!" The owner, Mrs. Hedford, smiled and wiped her hands on a towel. "Ready to make an appointment?"

"Yes, ma'am." I glanced at the appointment book on her desk. I could use a trim. "How about now?"

"Sounds perfect." She led me to a stylist chair and wrapped a plastic apron around me. "Just a reshape?"

"Yes. Brad likes my hair long."

"Of course, he does. It's thick and wavy. People would die to have hair like yours." She led me to the shampoo sink, chattering away about hair she'd cut. One of the things about visiting the salon was I didn't have to ask a lot of questions. Mrs. Hedford enjoyed hearing herself talk.

"Did you ever cut Mrs. Wells' hair?" I asked as she led me back to her station.

"Surprisingly, yes. She'd make the drive all the way here for me to cut her hair."

"One time, you weren't here," Sally, one of the other stylists, said, "and I had to cut it. She was not a happy woman. Difficult to please and threatened to have my license revoked."

"Really?" I swiveled in my chair, only to have Mrs. Hedford turn me back around. "She seemed so nice when she dropped her dog and cat off at Tail Waggin'. How long ago was this?"

"Last week. Right before someone knocked her off. If she was nice to you, it's because you hadn't slipped up yet."

I met Mrs. Hedford's surprised glance in the mirror. Sally didn't seem strong enough to choke a woman who outweighed her by thirty pounds, but anger gave strength.

"Don't be disrespectful of the dead, Sally." Mrs. Hedford started cutting my hair.

"I'm sorry, but she scared me. All because I took off a little too much." Sally burst into tears and darted to the back, leaving her client in the chair.

"She's a sensitive girl," Mrs. Hedford said.

"Temper?"

"No way. She resorts to tears when upset. Are you investigating again?"

"Just curious." I caught the interested expression of the client sitting in Sally's station. When she caught me looking, she ducked her head. "Did you know Mrs. Wells?"

The woman sniffed. "I certainly did. I cleaned her house. For pennies!"

"I take it you weren't fond of her."

"Most definitely not." She smiled when Sally returned. "Now focus, dear. A woman's hair is her crowning glory."

As I paid for my haircut, I quietly asked Mrs. Hedford the name of Sally's client. "That's Martha Grimes. You looking for a cleaner?"

"My apartment is too small. Thank you." I paid and left. Next stop, the thrift shop where I intended to be upfront.

I found the widow Murdoch hanging dresses on a rack. "Have you had things donated from a Mrs. Wells?"

"The poor lady who was killed?" Her brows rose. "I'm hanging them now. Her daughter dropped them off a couple of days ago. Why?"

The real question was why hadn't Valerie told me she was back in town. "Any jewelry?"

"Just some costume stuff, but it's all too old for a young lady like yourself."

"May I see the items?"

"Sure. They're still in the box. Costume pieces, not inexpensive. I'll have to put them in the locked case." She led me to the front counter where she pulled a box from behind, setting it where I could look.

"Did you know her?"

"Never met her. Her daughter was a chilly one, though."

"How so?" I lifted a chunky gold necklace from the box.

"At first, she thought I'd purchase the items from her and was peeved when I said all were donations, and that some of the proceeds go to the homeless shelter in Blytheville. She dropped everything on the counter and raced out of here as if her rear end was on fire. Busy woman, I guess. Why all the interest?"

"I'm helping her locate some missing items." A moot point since she was the one who donated the items in front of me. "Maybe you shouldn't mention to anyone that these came from a murdered woman's closet. Her daughter didn't drop off anything requiring a key, did she?" She hadn't notified me that she'd contacted the bank.

"No, but I found this in a coat pocket." She took a slip of paper from the cash register and handed it to me.

Bingo. The name of a bank in Blytheville and the box number. My biggest clue yet. "You're awesome."

I headed to the drugstore, but I highly doubted the Parkers would know Mrs. Wells since the deceased wouldn't come all the way to Waterfall for a prescription. Still, I refused to leave any stone unturned.

"Yes, we knew her quite well," Mrs. Parker said. "We attend the same church. The funeral is next week, you know."

"I didn't." Another question for Valerie. I'd be sure to be there since the killer often attended the services of their victim.

Same story at the bookstore/coffee shop. Mrs. Ansley attended church with the deceased.

"Was she well-liked within the congregation?"

Mrs. Ansley shrugged. "Seemed to be. I know the pastor really liked her. She donated a lot of money to the church. There's even a bench outside with her name on it." She handed me my order, the largest mocha drink she made. "Your handsome man hasn't been in for a while."

"He's out of town on business. Brad'll be back tomorrow." I couldn't wait. After our serious talk and heavy kissing a few nights before, he was my last thought at night and my first in the morning.

I returned to Tail Waggin' and let Heather and Shar know the details of my day. "Not a lot to go on, but some things to look into further."

"The bank box number is a great find," Shar said. "Not to mention Sally didn't like her and the upcoming funeral."

"Or the fact that Valerie hasn't let you know she's returned," Heather added. "Why don't you call and confront her?"

"I plan on it, as soon as we close for the day." The woman had some explaining to do. If she expected me to help her, she needed to be honest with me. By not doing so, she rose higher on my suspect list.

"Will the bank let you into the box?" Heather tilted her head.

"I'm hoping to find a way to talk my way in. Would be a lot easier if Valerie went with me, she being the heir."

"Ask her."

"I'm not sure I trust her."

After flipping the open sign to closed at five, I headed to my apartment, my three fur babies racing ahead of me in anticipation of being fed. After taking care of their needs, I dialed Valerie. "Why didn't you tell me you were in town?"

"I've been busy."

"You were right here at the thrift store. You could have popped in for a moment."

She laughed. "You sound like a jealous girlfriend."

"The thrift shop owner found a bank box number in the pocket of one of the coats. I'm heading over there in the morning. Do you want to come along?"

"I could go myself since you have work to do."

"No, I want to. My curiosity is aroused." Now, why would a woman who'd hired me to help her want to do things alone?

# Chapter Six

"You don't trust me." Valeria glared, arms crossed at me the next morning when I insisted on driving to the bank.

"There is some hesitation on my part." I slid into the driver's seat.

"Like what?"

"The fact you didn't tell me you were in town, for one." I started the car. "The fact you hired me to help, which I'm spending a lot of time doing, yet you still want to do things by yourself, for two."

"Not doing things on my own takes some getting used to. I'll try to do better." She stared out the passenger window as I drove to the bank in Blytheville.

Good thing she came with me because the bank refused to allow me access, even with the key, until Valerie produced her identification as her mother's only child. I supposed the bank was something she could've done without me, but I wanted to know every single detail of the missing jewels.

A frowning clerk led us to a room where slide-out boxes lined the walls. "Push that bell when you're finished, and I'll let you out."

"They must think this place is Fort Knox." I stepped back while Valerie slid out her mother's box.

She unlocked the box and opened the lid. "I was hoping for the missing jewelry."

I peered around her and stared at a plain white envelope. "Maybe she wrote you a letter."

"Why lock it up?"

"Open it." Anticipation bubbled like the champagne at the country club. What was so important that she wrote it down and put it in a safety deposit box?

"A love letter? No, wait..." Valerie's eyes darted from word to word. "A threat." She handed me the sheet of paper. "My mother's killer."

I started reading, "Bill. I won't say 'Dear, Bill,' because that would be an utter lie. What you've done to the people at Serenity Falls Nursing Home is an abomination. Oh, yes, I know exactly what you've done. I've also made a copy of this letter and put it in a safe place in case something happens to me. You will be coming for me, won't you?" I swallowed against a dry throat.

"To think that what I thought was love has to die like this. Mark my words, Bill. Your deeds will be found out, and you will pay. I'll make sure of it. Alice." I met Valerie's startled gaze. "She knew he'd come and kill her. I wish she'd given us more information than just a first name. Do you know who she's talking about?"

She shook her head. "Mom never told me she was seeing anyone, but like I've told you, we weren't close the last few years." When I went to hand her the letter, she held her palm up. "I need to head back to the city You keep it. Let me know if you find out anything." She left the box on the table and set the key beside it. "I'll be back in a week or so, but I'll call you for updates." A flicker of sadness crossed her face. "Stay close to your mother, Trinity. She won't always be around."

"She's gallivanting around Europe with my father. Has been for over a year." I didn't grudge them their fun. They'd worked their entire lives for this trip, but I did miss them. It had been a long time since we'd talked to each other. "Most of the time, they're out of cell service."

"Figure it out." She pressed the button signaling we were ready to leave.

After I dropped Valerie off, I sat in my car and tried calling my parents. Voice mail. "Mom, I miss you. I know I told you I'd only call once a month, but you never return my calls. Let me know you and Dad are okay, please. Love you."

Surprisingly, I got an immediate response via text.

Deep in mud baths, sweetie. We're fine. Love you. Do try and stay alive until we return next month. We keep tabs on the local news. You've been very busy.

Of course, they kept tabs. I laughed, missing them more than ever. They'd know all about my business, Brad, and the crimes I'd helped solve. I could hear the lecturing already.

Still grinning, I entered Tail Waggin' and let my friends know what Valerie and I had found. "Now to find out who Bill is."

"Let's head over to the nursing home after work," Shar said. "What time does Brad get home?"

"Around seven, I think. That gives us some time. Will they let us just waltz in and start asking questions?" I didn't think so. "We could say we want to volunteer."

She shuddered. "Heaven forbid."

"Fine. I'll volunteer. You keep on being Selfish Shar." I scratched Sheba behind the ears. "I'll take you along. I bet those folks would love some Sheba kisses."

"I'll go with you. Maybe they'll have volunteer work I won't mind doing."

"Like what?" I raised my brows.

"I won't know until I go." With a toss of her hair, she headed to the grooming room.

"We have some kittens to sell." Heather leaned on the counter. "Why not take one or two with you for the people to snuggle with? My grandmother said they always enjoyed it when people brought in pets or children."

"Great idea." I actually looked forward to the visit and called the nursing home to make sure it was okay to visit and bring the animals. Assured that it was, I got to work.

At five on the dot, Shar and I left with a basket of kittens and Sheba, leaving Heather to lock up. "Be nice," I told Shar. "You might actually have fun."

"I'm not a fan of those places."

"Someday you might be in one."

"That's what I'm afraid of."

When we arrived, she took the basket of kittens while I kept a firm grip on Sheba's leash. My dog had responded very well to her training, but at a year old, new places still excited her a little too much.

The woman at the reception desk, Ann, according to her name tag, was excited to see us and gushed over Sheba and the kittens. "Everyone is in the dining hall right now. You're welcome to go on in. Even eat with them if you'd like. It's meat-loaf night."

"She sounds excited about meat loaf," Shar whispered.

"Shh." I kept a smile on my face and followed Ann into a room that reminded me of my high school cafeteria. Round tables and a mixture of aromas. This time ground beef and talcum powder instead of pizza and cologne.

Ann clapped her hands to get everyone's attention. "We have visitors. Isn't that wonderful? They're going to eat with you, and they've brought furry friends." She glanced at me. "Set the kittens on that table over there and let your dog off the leash. She'll be fine."

Multiple hands immediately held out snippets of food to entice Sheba to their table. My dog would be in heaven.

I set the basket on the appointed table but didn't have it open before eager people reached for one. "You'll have to share. I only have four." The kittens would be completely socialized by the time we left.

"What a darling," one woman said, tucking the calico kitten under her chin.

At Ann's insistence that we eat, Shar and I headed for the buffet and filled our plates with the simple fare of meatloaf, mashed potatoes, green beans, and a roll. "Just like what they served at school," I said. "Without the choice of pizza."

Shar eyed her plate. "I hope it tastes better than it looks."

"Hush and find a table to sit at." I spotted one with an empty chair and sat next to two men and one woman. One of the men slipped half his roll to Sheba.

"I'm Trinity." I smiled at each one around the table. "The lady I came with is Shar." I motioned to where she'd sat at a different table.

"Margie, Hank, and Frank," my female companion said. "They're brothers."

"I'm Hank, that's Frank." Hank glared as his brother took the last bit of meatloaf off Hank's plate and fed it to Sheba. "Feed the dog your own food."

"I'm hungry. You said you were full two seconds ago."

"That's before we had a guest." Hank crossed his arms.

I chuckled and bit into my meat loaf, surprised at how tasty it was. "I can bring pets on a regular basis. I own a pet store and daycare." Maybe I could persuade some of the pet owners to agree to me bringing my daycare pets on a field trip. It would break up the animals' day and brighten the lives of some elderly people.

"I heard some of y'all got scammed a while

back." I dipped my fork into my potatoes.

"Yep," Frank said. "Not me, though. I was too smart to fall for the whole smart watch thing."

"Smart watch?" My hand paused halfway to my mouth.

He nodded. "Some fella tried selling these watches that would keep track of our heart rate and breathing…that sort of stuff, but they didn't do a bit of good. Why Homer died in his sleep, but the watch told the front desk—everything was on an app, you see?—Anyway, the information sent to the desk said his heart was still beating. Upon further investigation, they determined that everyone's hearts beat at the same rate whether they could walk or were in a wheelchair."

I wasn't sure what sort of scam I'd expected, but it definitely wasn't this. "A pretty involved scam. How many of you bought the watches? Why didn't the nursing home buy them?"

"One question at a time, dearie. I'm old." Frank wiped his mouth, then tossed his napkin on his plate. "Not everyone wanted one. Some of us don't trust this new technology, me for one. Hank did, though. He even walked faster down the hall to see if his heart rate would speed up. All he got for his efforts was an asthma attack. As for the home, well, they can't afford such an expense. The watches cost two hundred each. The scoundrel made four-thousand dollars off these people."

I'd have to call other nursing homes in the area to see whether this Bill guy was still pushing the scam. If he was, we could catch him easily enough. "That's awful."

"A damn shame."

"Did you know this man's name?"

"I have his card." Margie pulled a business card from a crocheted bag. "I keep everything."

Printed on the plain white card were the words Bill's Healthy Technology and a phone number. "Do you have a pen I can borrow?"

Margie handed me a pink glittery one, and I wrote the phone number on my napkin. "Thanks." While I doubted the number was valid, I'd call it anyway.

After supper, Shar and I gathered up the kittens with promises to return in a few days. Sheba gave a lingering look back as we headed for my car.

"Come on, we'll return." I turned to Shar. "That wasn't so bad, was it? An hour of your time to make some folks happy?"

"No, and the food wasn't horrible. I did receive three marriage proposals, though." She laughed. "That place was good for my ego. Terrible about the scam, though. How do you think Wells found out about it?"

"Maybe she bought one of those watches." I called to ask Valerie if I could go back into the house.

"Sure. Everything is still there, minus the jewelry and the costume stuff I took to the thrift store."

Right. I'd head to Someone Else's Junk and see whether a smart watch had been in the box with the other costume jewelry.

We'd find this Bill and put him behind bars for the murder of Alice Wells.

# TROUBLESOME TWOSOME

# Chapter Seven

The next morning, Mrs. Murdoch was more than happy to oblige and pulled a watch from under the thrift store counter. "No one had expressed any interest in this."

"Because it's fake." I glared at the item that looked every bit as impressive as one that worked. "I wonder how Alice discovered the truth?"

"Maybe she visited Serenity Falls and compared her watch to someone else's," Shar said. "She's no dummy."

True. I sighed and handed the watch back. "I'd toss it in the garbage if I were you. It's no good."

"Pity. I thought I could get thirty-dollars for it." Mrs. Murdoch shoved it to the side. "I'll put it in with the cheap stuff. It does tell time, at least."

Outside, I leaned against the warm concrete wall. "If we can't locate this Bill person, we're back to the beginning." I dialed the number on the business card I'd been given. It went straight to a recording. "Yes, hello, this is Trinity Ashford. I'd like to speak with you regarding your smart watch." I left my phone number and hung up.

Either he'd call me back, or the man would know how nosy I was and try to stop me from snooping around. While I hoped he'd call me back, I doubted he would. Anyone around Waterfall knew my talent for being nosy. I could find myself in danger again, but the money would be worth getting involved again. Find Bill and find the missing items.

Shar and I returned to the store and filled Heather in on how happy the animals had made the residents of Serenity Falls. She smiled and clapped her hands. "I hope we always have fur babies to take. Your idea of using boarding animals is a good one."

I nodded. "We'll make sure they're sociable first, find vaccine records…I'd hate someone to get bitten." I took my place behind the counter and pulled up the monthly reports. I loved that Tail Waggin stayed in the black, and it didn't bother me that I'd set aside my dream of becoming a veterinarian. My life was fuller than I'd ever thought it could be. Busier, too. Sometimes, dreams changed, and I was living mine to the fullest.

The bell jingled over the door, and Brad strolled in. A smile graced his handsome face.

"I missed you." I jumped up and rushed his way, relieving him of the four coffees in his hand.

"Me or the coffee?" He arched a brow.

"I'm emptying your hands so you can kiss me." I smiled and set the drinks on the counter before wrapping my arms around his neck. After a short, sweet kiss, since we were in front of a large glass window, I moved back and asked, "Can you visit for a few minutes? I'd like to fill you in on my last few days."

"Sure." He sat at the table and listened as I talked. When I'd finished, he remained quiet for a minute, then spoke. "Bill is a common name. Have you asked around whether Alice Wells was seen with a man? The letter does say she thought she loved him."

"Not yet. I've been so busy after finding out about the watches that I haven't focused on anything else." I sipped my coffee. "I can make the rounds of those here in the mall again, then attend her church. Folks there might know something. The funeral is this week, too."

"Have you shown the letter to Prentiss?"

I shuddered. "No, but I guess I have to. Otherwise, I'm guilty of withholding evidence, and the last thing I want is for him to throw me in jail."

After Brad left, I drove to the police station with all the enthusiasm of a convicted man heading to the gas chamber. I parked in front of the building, then plodded toward the front glass door. The letter, which I'd made a copy of, crackled in my back pocket.

Inside, I approached the reception desk and asked for Officer Prentiss. "When will McIlroy be returning?"

"Tomorrow." She reached for the phone on her desk and let Prentiss know I was there. "He said to go on back."

If I were going to see McIlroy, I might be able

to find out where the police were on investigating Mrs. Wells' murder. Prentiss wouldn't be as obliging.

"You have something for me?" Prentiss glared as I entered, his arms crossed. "Are you meddling in my investigation?"

I fought the urge to roll my eyes. "I found a key in Mrs. Wells' cat's collar. Remember how she liked to hide her jewels in weird places? Anyway, her daughter and I went to the bank and found a letter in the safety deposit box. That isn't against the law, is it?" I handed him the letter.

"Considering it's you, it probably is." He read the letter. "Who's Bill?"

"I have no idea." I explained the complaints of the Serenity Hall residents.

"So, you are meddling," he practically growled.

"I was volunteering." I narrowed my eyes. "People like to talk to me. You hand them a cuddly baby animal, and they'll tell you almost anything. You should try it sometime. How are things on your end?"

"None of your business. I'm a busy man, Miss Ashford. Anything else?"

"Nope." I wouldn't tell him another thing unless absolutely necessary. "Since you seem to be having a difficult time finding Mrs. Wells' killer, it must be a relief to know Detective McIlroy is returning tomorrow." I flashed a sassy grin and left him with a red face.

Since Mr. and Mrs. Parker attended church with Alice, I headed there first. "Did Alice ever attend church with a man?"

Mrs. Parker wrinkled her nose in thought. "Not that I ever saw. She did bring a friend once, someone named Irma, but only once."

Ah, the woman who now had her pets. "Thanks." Next stop the hair salon. If Alice had a boyfriend, she might have told the one styling her hair. Women liked telling their stylists about their personal lives.

The owner wasn't there but Sally was. "I never heard her say anything about a man."

"Did she ever wear a smart watch?"

Sally took a couple more cuts on the woman seated in the chair in front of her before answering. "I do seem to recall her wearing one toward the end of her life, but I don't think she did the last time she was here. You need to remember that I'm not her stylist. Unless I overhear something—"

"I understand. Thanks." I left with no new information. This case was going to be a tough one to crack.

I spotted a squad car parked outside Tail Waggin'. My heart dropped to my knees as Prentiss climbed out and waited for me.

"Asking questions?"

"Is visiting the drugstore and hair salon a crime now?"

"I'm watching you, Miss Ashford. Don't do anything stupid."

"I'm flattered that you came out here to tell me that." I grinned. "A simple phone call would have done the job."

"I've been to the nursing home. An old woman told me she gave you a business card." He held out his hand. "It was the last one."

"Oh. No problem." I fished the card from my pocket. "Sorry about that."

"No evidence is too small." His eyes practically shot sparks. He climbed back into his car and drove away.

I really missed McIlroy. He, at least, accepted my help, albeit begrudgingly sometimes.

"Tomorrow?" Shar's face lit up. "I'll make sure to look my best. He's bound to come in here to see what you've discovered."

"He hasn't asked me to get involved."

"No, but Valerie did." Shar smiled and greeted a grooming customer, a beautiful silver toy poodle. "I'll have this darling ready by four this afternoon," she told the owner. With a spring in her step, she carried the dog to the grooming room.

Out of curiosity, I did an internet search on Office Prentiss. The man had been accused of police brutality and reassigned after his suspension. Had they sent him to our town in the hope that a smaller place would offer fewer chances for confrontation?

Could I use that information to convince him to stop trying to keep me from doing what I'd been hired to do? Would obtaining a private investigator's license work? My questions about Prentiss clouded my brain, making it harder to think about the murder and missing jewelry pieces. I needed to concentrate on what was important—doing what Valerie had hired me for.

McIlroy entered the shop a few minutes before closing.

"The receptionist said tomorrow. I can't believe I'm telling you this, but we've missed you."

"I'm back to work tomorrow." He laughed. "Prentiss is hard to get used to." He glanced through the glass separating us from the grooming station. "Why is Shar ducking behind a table?"

"She doesn't look her best." I chuckled. "Do you want me to bring her out here?"

"No, it's you I want to speak with. I don't have to ask whether you're snooping."

"Mrs. Wells' daughter hired me to find the missing pieces of jewelry." I told him about finding the items in strange places, the letter in the safety deposit box, and the smart-watches scam. "Mrs. Murdoch has the watch that belonged to Mrs. Wells, but I left it. It's not worth anything."

He rubbed his chin in an attempt to hide a grin, occasionally glancing past me. I didn't want to know what antics Shar was up to.

"Prentiss keeps threatening me with arrest." I straightened in my chair. "I haven't done anything illegal. Not even breaking and entering. Well, except for going into Mrs. Wells' home to search for the jewels, but I was with her daughter."

"I'll handle Prentiss. He hasn't learned what an asset you are in helping our small department."

"I don't think he'll care." I almost brought up the officer's past but decided not to. McIlroy would already know. "The funeral is tomorrow. Oh, and these are the contacts from Mrs. Wells' phone. Her daughter wrote them down for me. I've already questioned everyone here in the strip mall, and while the woman wasn't particularly liked, I don't think any of them killed her."

"Does Prentiss know about this?"

I shook my head. "I forgot."

"Okay. You just received this and passed it to me right away. Understand?"

"Got it. Welcome back."

He glanced over my shoulder again. "See you at the funeral, Shar."

"Why couldn't he arrive when he was supposed to?" Shar joined me in the front. "I had dog shampoo in my hair." She set the poodle in the dog playpen. "I've never been more mortified in my life."

"McIlroy couldn't keep his eyes off you," Heather said. "I watched from where I stocked shelves. He might have been speaking to Trinity, but it was you he stared at."

Shar patted her hair and smiled. "Yeah, I also noticed he wasn't quite as grouchy as usual. The man definitely needed a vacation. Maybe he'll take me on his next one." She wiggled her brows. "Who will watch the store tomorrow? I want to attend the funeral. The killer will definitely be there."

"I will," Heather said. "I had enough excitement a few months ago to last a lifetime." Her cheeks pinkened.

"You have a secret." I narrowed my eyes. "Spill."

"I have a date with David tonight."

"It's about time." I clapped.

"Great." Shar glowered. "She gets a date with a handsome man while I play detective with Trinity. Life is so unfair."

# Chapter Eight

The parking lot of the funeral home was packed. Since Mrs. Wells didn't seem very well liked, I assumed the place would be full of looky-loos, people curious about her murder.

I slipped my hand in Brad's and joined the line of people filing inside the building. A yoo-hoo from behind us stopped me. I turned, my eyes widening as Shar, dressed in black sparkling pants and a gauzy blouse that billowed around her, rushed toward us. "What are you wearing?"

"Black, as is fitting for a funeral." She patted her hair. "I wanted to look good for McIlroy."

"We're here to pay our respects not hook up."

"And find a killer. Don't forget that." She tapped my arm. "Don't get distracted from our original goal."

"*You* should remember." I shook my head and continued with Brad into the building, taking note of everyone there. A lot I knew, like those from the strip mall, but many I didn't. I slipped free of Brad with promises to catch up to him when the service started.

"Be careful. I see a business associate I need to speak with." He kissed my cheek and headed in the opposite direction.

McIlroy stood just inside the room by the door with Prentiss on the other side of the door. A pair of bookends came to mind. Officer Rickson stood at the front of the room. Shar and I weren't the only ones expecting the killer to show.

Shar smiled and waved at McIlroy whose gaze flickered her way. He took a double take, then resumed his stoic stare forward. Satisfied at having caught his attention, Shar followed me to the other room where a table with cookies, tea, and lemonade had been set up.

Spotting Irma, I headed her way. "How are Honey and Prince?"

She frowned. "Into everything, those two. And I don't dare separate them. It makes things worse. I have no idea how Alice coped."

"Unfortunately, I have a feeling they only behaved for her." Poor things must miss their human. "It's only a matter of time before they realize they belong to you now."

"I hope I survive that long." She narrowed her eyes to where Sally and a young man whispered together in the corner. "Excuse me."

I waited a few seconds and subtly followed her, pretending to pause until I was standing a few feet from her, Sally, and the young man.

"William, I asked you to behave yourself and not attract attention," Irma hissed.

"I'm only talking." His face darkened.

"The two of you are snuggled up like you're at a party. Remember why you're here and fade into the background."

I turned my back to the trio as Irma left—an interesting conversation considering I didn't see the young people doing anything inappropriate. Heads bent together to have a quiet conversation didn't seem so bad.

"My mother is a dragon." William took Sally's arm and dragged her away.

"We aren't supposed to leave, Willy," Sally said.

I didn't hear the rest of their conversation since they were now too far away, but the tone suggested an imminent argument. I caught Prentiss watching me and tossed him a sarcastic salute, no longer worried in the slightest about making him mad. McIlroy was his superior and knew my worth in getting information out of people.

I weaved in and out of the throng and joined the Parkers. "Quite the crowd."

Mrs. Parker frowned. "People always flock to the macabre. That woman you were talking to earlier is the one who attended church with Alice."

"They are friends. In fact, she took Alice's pets rather than leave them for strangers to adopt." I scanned the room for Brad, knowing the preacher would approach the podium soon. "Her name is Irma Grable."

Mrs. Parker nodded. "Alice introduced us at church. Her friend wasn't any friendlier than Alice. In fact, the two seemed to have some sort of disagreement after church. I heard them arguing in the parking lot."

"We shouldn't gossip, dear." Mr. Parker took his wife's hand and led her away.

But, I wanted the gossip. I'd learned there was always an element of truth in gossip. All a person had to do was dig deep enough to find that nugget.

Brad waved for me to join him, then slid into a back row. "I thought you'd want to watch everyone's reaction." A crooked grin spread over his face.

"You know me so well." I hugged his arm, then straightened as Shar sat on the other side of me.

"I have some news," she whispered.

"After the ceremony."

Valerie sat in the front row, pale-faced, back straight. It seemed her mother's death meant more than she'd originally let on. Brad had told me when he'd picked me up that morning that a get together would be held in the banquet room he'd added to the theater. He was always looking for ways to make more money, and there was a need for a glamorous place to hold wedding receptions and such.

Once that had bothered me. Now, I took advantage of his financial genius and implemented some of the same ideas in my business. Like the grooming van. It was definitely time to get Shar on the road.

The preacher took his place behind the podium, drawing my attention back to where it should be. He spoke about how influential Alice had been in her community, a regular church-going woman, a generous donor to local charities…more like a shopping list than a person who would be missed because they were loved.

My throat clogged. How sad. I wanted people to miss me fir who I was and how I'd contributed emotionally to making their lives better, not because of my money.

Sensing my mood, Brad gave my hand a gentle squeeze. "Don't worry. Everyone in Waterfall would miss you if you were gone."

The preacher wrapped things up, and those in attendance lined up to approach the coffin. He informed everyone about the reception at the Waterfall theater's banquet room after the burial.

"It always amazes me how well the makeup people cover up wounds," Shar whispered from behind me in the line. "You can't see where she was shot."

"Shh." I glanced around, praying no one had heard her. "If they can't hide it, it's closed casket." I said a prayer for Alice and her daughter, then followed Brad from the building.

We drove to the cemetery where a large marble headstone towered over a freshly dug hole. I went to Valerie's side. She stood and stared as men carried the oak casket to the grave. "I thought Mom would like a grand headstone."

"I think you're right." I put my hand on her shoulder. "We'll find out who did this. I promise."

She heaved a sigh, then choked back a sob. "It's not even about the necklace and tiara anymore. Seeing her lying there in that casket, well, what I want right now is justice."

I vowed to make sure she got just that. There weren't as many people at the cemetery as the funeral home, but they'd be waiting at the reception hall for the free food. Brad had declined Valerie's offer to pay, saying he refused to take money from a grieving daughter. I had a feeling all funeral receptions would be on the house.

Sure enough, the parking lot in front of the theater was full. A crowd waited by the side door that led to the banquet hall.

Inside, I hunted up Shar. "What's your news?"

She led me to a corner. "I found this on the floor."

I stared at the same business card Frank had given me. The one with Bill's name. "Do you think McIlroy or Prentiss dropped it?"

"They wouldn't be that careless. No, Bill is here and still trying to sell his bogus watches."

It did make sense. Why not work an available crowd? "Keep your eyes and ears open. Let's find this creep."

"At least we know we're looking for a man." Shar grabbed a glass of sparkling water from a nearby tray and slipped into the crowd. Amazing what a woman who dressed to attract attention could find out by simply skirting a group of people.

I went in search of Valerie and handed her the business card. "Ring a bell?"

"Nope. You should probably let the police know the man is here." She sipped a soda. "I'd like to round up all the men and make them talk."

Me too. "I'll turn this over and do some scouting."

A muscle ticked in McIlroy's jaw as he glanced at the card. "So the suspect is here." His hard gaze roamed the crowd. "Keep mingling. Give me a sign if you find anyone that might be this Bill person."

"You're actually having a civilian get involved in a murder case?" Prentiss's brows lowered so far his eyes almost disappeared.

"People talk to Trinity, Officer. We aren't getting anywhere on our own." McIlroy slipped the card into his pocket.

With a curt nod toward Prentiss, I headed in the opposite direction Shar had gone. I kept my ears open for anyone introduced as Bill. Two rounds later and nada. I plopped onto a chair. What was I missing?

Shar joined me. "I got nothing."

"Same here."

"I did meet a few Williams, though."

"What?"

"Bill is often short for William." She pointed out three men, plus Sally's boyfriend. "The young man goes by Willy, according to that silly girl. But the others introduced themselves as William. See what kind of information you can get when you dress up?" She eyed my simple black dress.

"There is nothing wrong with my dress. I've worn it to the country club and fit in fine."

"Sometimes, you need a little more. I'm going to go talk with our Williams and find out who is interested in smart watches. Maybe make McIlroy jealous in the process." She grinned and took off.

I doubted that, since he knew we were searching for information, but I left my friend to her delusions. The three men named William seemed rather pleased with Shar's flirtations, and I enjoyed the entertainment.

"Are you Shar's friend?" A man around the age of thirty approached me, a folder in his hand.

"Yes, I'm Trinity Ashford."

"I've done some more digging into the list of names Shar gave me." He handed me the folder.

"I thought you'd be older."

He laughed. "My father is her ex. I thought I'd done enough digging, but after reading about the murder in the newspaper, I'm behind, so I thought I'd do some more. Let me know what you need."

"Thank you." I itched to study the papers I held, though I still hadn't questioned anyone on the list other than the other store owners of Waterfall Mall. Maybe this new information would help me set my priorities.

"What's that?" Prentiss stopped in front of me.

"Paperwork." I put on my most innocent expression.

"May I see?" He held out his hand.

"No, sir, it's personal." I tightened my grip on the folder. While I had every intention of turning the papers over to McIlroy, I still had to make copies. "Excuse me." I rushed away from him and up a flight of stairs to the theater office.

Locking the door behind me, I copied the pages and stored them in the desk. I could retrieve them after the reception. Folder in hand, I returned downstairs and headed to McIlroy and Prentiss. "I changed my mind. Here is some more information on the people on Alice Wells' contact list."

I squared my shoulders and did my best not to flinch at the hard look in Prentiss's eyes. If I wasn't careful, I'd find myself on the wrong end of his alleged police brutality.

"Watch yourself, Miss Ashford," he growled, moving past me. His bump to my shoulder caused me to stumble.

McIlroy's face hardened as he reached out to steady me.

# Chapter Nine

Since Heather had been covering the store for me a lot recently, I gave her the next day off. Brad had come and gone with my coffee, Shar called in to say she'd be late, and I spotted Honey and Prince online for sale. I sighed and called Irma. At least she hadn't taken them to the pound. Yet.

"The cat has shredded my curtains, and the dog chewed the corner of my leather sofa. I cannot keep them." Irma's anger vibrated over the phone.

"Are they alone a lot?"

"Of course, they are. I'm a busy woman."

"Perhaps you'd consider my daycare for them?" I cringed at the thought of watching the Troublesome Twosome, but who knew where they'd end up. I doubted Irma would check out the prospective owners to see whether they were able to properly care for the animals.

"I suppose that's an option." Irma huffed. "Fine. I'll drop them off within the hour and remove the ad. For now." Click.

"Why do you look like someone kicked Sheba?" Shar entered the store and set her purse in the locked drawer behind the counter.

"Honey and Prince will be staying with us during the day."

"Oh boy." She palmed her forehead. "Best keep them locked up."

"Except for exercise, I will." Although I hated to lock them up, they'd destroy my store in no time. "I'm going to recommend the dog trainer who helped me with Sheba. If Irma can train Honey to behave, maybe the cat will follow suit."

"Wishful thinking. That's the glory of cats. They do what they want, and we still love them."

"It's time to start the mobile grooming service." I pulled the stack of papers from my bag regarding Alice's contact list. "Some of the daycare doggies will still need their grooming appointments, but I'm sure you can work around their schedule."

"Yay. I'll make up an advertisement right away and ensure the van is ready for business." She rushed to the back of the store and into the alley where the van was parked. I did like her enthusiasm.

Before I could dig into the papers, Irma rushed in with Honey on a leash and Prince in a padded cat carrier. "I thought he'd be more comfortable in this, but he still howls as if someone has set his tail on fire." Her gaze dropped to the stack of papers. "That's a lot of paperwork."

I set a file on top. "Unfortunately, running a business requires it."

"Yes, I know. I'm a business...well, I'd best be

getting along." She turned.

"Did you know Alice long?"

She faced me. "Only a few months, but given time, we'd have been the best of friends."

"The service was nice." I wasn't quite sure why I kept talking, but Irma was one of Alice's contacts, and she was right in front of me. Asking questions now would prevent me from making a phone call later.

"Yes." She glanced over her shoulder at the door, then at her watch.

"Your son seems like a nice young man."

"He's a scoundrel. I really am in a hurry, Trinity. See you later." She rushed away before I could say anything else.

I collected Honey from where she'd started chewing through a bag of dog treats and carried both her and the carrier to the kennels. "Don't worry, you two. I'm putting you together. Darn. I forgot to tell Irma about the trainer." I'd slip a business card in the cat carrier.

When I returned to the front of the store, I spotted Irma heading across the parking lot. Had she come back in for something? I glanced at the counter. The folder I'd placed across the stack of papers looked askew. Was it my imagination? I stared at Irma as she slid into a black Cadillac. Why would she be so interested in my paperwork?

"What?" Shar joined me, loaded down with cleaning supplies.

I explained what I'd seen.

"She probably forgot something, but if I were you, I'd keep that stuff hidden. Who knows what woman around these parts knows the Bill we're looking for?"

True. I didn't want the man tipped off until we discovered his identity.

The rest of the day passed as usual. Some mixed-breed puppies were dropped off which I'd take to entertain the seniors at Serenity, several customers reserved boarding times and bought pet supplies. Granted, some of them were people wanting to know details of the funeral, but a sale was a sale.

Five o'clock rolled around but no Irma. I had a strange sense of déjà vu, remembering the same thing happening with Alice. I approved Shar's advertisement for the mobile grooming we'd be offering, went over prices with her, then loaded Honey and Prince in my car—all this, and Irma still hadn't arrived. Perhaps, I needed to start charging extra when people were late picking up their pets.

My head was pounding by the time I arrived at Irma's. Leash in one hand, carrier in the other, I climbed the stairs to a house smaller than Alice's but still a grand Victorian. The door swung open at my knock. Ants scurried up my spine. I'd definitely experienced this a time or two. "Irma?"

I stepped inside. Chairs overturned, a vase smashed, papers strewn.

After securing the animals in the bathroom, I called McIlroy. "I'm at Irma Grable's house and it looks like a break-in."

"Why are you there?"

"Returning her pets because she didn't show by closing time. I gave her an extra half hour."

"Have you found a body?"

"I haven't gone past the bathroom yet."

"Stay put." He hung up.

Right. Like I'd stay in the front room without knowing whether Irma was lying injured in another room.

A quick peek into the kitchen revealed cupboards hanging open but no sign of Irma. I checked a room used as an office. More vandalism. Then, I climbed the sweeping staircase, praying I wouldn't find her dead like I had Alice.

Had Irma recognized a name on the contact list and informed that person? Then had she been eliminated as a potential witness? I clutched the stair railing hard enough to make my knuckles ache. My footsteps sounded abnormally loud on the wooden floor. From downstairs came the sound of barking and the growls of an unhappy cat. Upstairs, nothing but my footsteps sounded as I crept toward double doors.

No body. Blankets on the floor, closet open, drawers dumped. Someone had searched for something. The question was...did they find what they hunted for?

Relieved not to find Irma, I headed downstairs and waited for McIlroy on the front porch. I frowned to see Prentiss with him. The officer was like a painful cold sore that kept popping up on my lip. "No body," I said.

"Must be a first for you." Prentiss strode past me and into the house.

I stopped McIlroy before he followed and told him about Irma's visit to the store and how it seemed as if she'd returned when I was in the back. I then told him my theory.

"Of course, you made copies." He exhaled as if I was a cold sore. "But, your theory is a good one. Go home, Trinity. We'll take it from here." He stopped and listened for a second. "What about the animals?"

"Guess I'll take them back to the kennels." I retrieved them again and headed back to the store. I'd spend my evening digging through those papers if it took me until two a.m.

By the time I had Honey and Prince fed and secured, Brad arrived with a bucket of fried chicken and all the fixin's. "You're the best boyfriend ever." I gave him a kiss and laughed as my stomach growled, awakened by the delectable odor coming from the bucket.

"I do my best. Want to watch a movie?" He set the food on the kitchen table.

"No. Want to help me look for a Bill or someone else in all the sordid details in that stack of papers?" I motioned to where I'd set them.

"That sounds more entertaining than any movie."

I handed him plates from the cupboard, then made sure my own fur babies had food and fresh water. Poor Sheba peered up at me with sad eyes as I took a seat at the table. "I know, sweetie. I've been neglecting you. Tomorrow I'll take you to the park, I promise." I smiled at Brad. "Want Alice's pets back?"

"I'd take the dog, but I swear the cat is the instigator. Since they shouldn't be separated, I'll decline." He grinned and handed me a plate piled with food. "So, we're looking for a Bill who sells phony smart watches. That will be like searching for a diamond in a bucket of crushed ice."

"No cube unturned and all that." I slid half the pile toward him. "Happy reading."

"Wow." His eyes widened. "Did you know the Parkers are really married?"

"They wear rings."

"Must have said some words themselves. Never applied for a license." He set their paper aside. "Maybe we should focus on people who own their own business."

"Why?" I bit into the crunchy skin of a chicken breast.

"Because they might have formed a corporation in order to sell the watches."

I grinned. "Love the way your financial brain works." I picked up my first sheet and started reading. Shar's friend's son was thorough. It seemed the only thing missing about Evans, the man who opened a gym next to Tail Waggin', was his blood type.

Married three times, no kids, filed for bankruptcy seven years ago. Nothing that pointed to him being a Bill. I didn't know the next person I read about, but since he was now in prison, I felt pretty sure we could discount him. Since Heather's divorce, we couldn't very well have her ex-husband ask questions for us anymore.

The next one was a William Mason. A sixty-year-old man, widowed, three grown children, with nothing more criminal on his record than unpaid parking tickets. I started to feel like we were wasting our time.

Sheba laid her head on my leg. I rubbed her ears, letting the solace she offered ease the stress of the day.

Brad's brow furrowed. "You said Honey's owner's home was vandalized?"

"Yes." I tilted my head.

"Is this her address?" He showed me her paper.

"No."

"Either she owns two houses or you were sent to the wrong place." He continued to read. "Irma's also a business owner under Grable Enterprises. She sells items on consignment."

"Like a thrift store?"

"An online one." He rolled his head on his shoulders. "Maybe this Bill asked her to sell his watches."

"Maybe she rents out the house on that paper." A whole lot of maybes.

"Easy enough to find out. I can check it out for you tomorrow."

"That'd be nice." I returned to stroking my dog's head, lifting a biscuit to my mouth with the other hand.

"My eyes are starting to cross." Brad stood. "I'll finish with Irma when I'm done eating. I haven't found anything to raise suspicion so far."

"Neither have I." As Brad headed for the bathroom down my short hallway, I pulled Irma's sheet toward me and scanned the information on the second page. The biscuit stuck in my throat. I forced it down with a gulp of iced tea.

When Brad returned, I handed him the page. "Irma's full name is Irma *Billie* Grable."

# Chapter Ten

The night before, Brad and I let McIlroy know about Irma's real name, but he already knew. He also know that Irma owned two houses. Unfortunately, the young couple renting one of them didn't know anything, according to McIlroy. Now, I sat on a bench by the lake tossing a ball for Sheba to fetch.

I'd had a hard time focusing on work that day, despite the shenanigans of Honey and Prince. Where was Irma? Had she fled Waterfall, or was she lying in wait to pounce? Was her son her accomplice? No one could find him—not even Sally, according to McIlroy. Which to me sounded like mother and son were a team. I needed to find out whether the Bill who had shown his face at Serenity Falls was a youngster or an older man.

"Come, Sheba." I'd take her and the new puppies to the nursing home, brighten some hearts, and maybe discover something valuable. I sent Brad a text letting him know where I was going, then drove to the home.

"You must be Trinity." A volunteer I hadn't met greeted me. "The residents ask every day when you're coming back. They've had their dinner and are now digging into dessert." She peered into the box I held. "Oh, puppies!"

Feeling pleased with myself for coming, I entered the cafeteria to applause. A girl couldn't help but get a bit of a big head with folks being so glad to see her and her four-legged friends. The pups left my side immediately in search of handouts. I scooped them up and headed straight for the table with Margie, Hank, and Frank. "I'm glad to see the three of you are well."

"Hank had a spell with his heart," Frank said, "but we're tough old birds, and he pulled through all right."

I pulled a business card from my pocket. "Please call me if you need anything at all." I definitely didn't want to show up at the home to find one of my new friends gone.

"You find that nincompoop, Bill, yet?" Hank asked.

"Not yet, but we have identified him, we think. Was he a young man or older?"

Margie cackled. "Anyone under forty is considered young to us. I'd say this Bill was maybe that age?"

"Not nineteen or twenty?" I frowned.

"Definitely not."

My shoulders slumped. It wasn't Irma or Willy who visited the home. Irma must have another accomplice. Was he also named Bill or only using that name?

"Cheer up, doll," Frank said. "We've followed the news articles about you. You'll get him."

"Do y'all have friends in other homes? Hear about them talking about the watch scam?"

Margie tapped her forefinger against her lips. "I haven't heard, but I have a cousin I can call. She's the nosiest person in the joint. If they were scammed, she'll know." She took my business card and slipped it into the pocket of her housedress.

I stayed another half hour, then rounded up the rowdy puppies and Sheba and returned to the store. As always I parked in the alley and carried the puppies through the backdoor and into the front. I froze.

Display cases were knocked over. The trash can sat precariously on top of the cages I'd installed for pets for sale. Papers and receipts littered the floor.

I put the puppies away and scooped my cat into my arms, glancing around for Sharkbait. "Here, kitty kitty."

He slunk around the corner of the storage room. Tears filled my eyes. I called Brad. "Someone broke into Tail Waggin'." I sniffed.

"On my way. Get out of the store." Click.

With a cat under each arm, I thundered up the stairs to my apartment, Sheba on my heels. The same sight greeted me there. I shouldn't have been surprised. You breach either the top or bottom floor, and you have easy access to the other.

After shutting the cats in the bedroom, I called for Sheba to follow me outside. I sat on the curb and waited, calling McIlroy as I did.

"Be right there." Click.

I doubted whoever broke in lingered in the area. Not finding what they wanted, they'd have gone away. Good thing I now carried the contact sheets in the bag I kept in my vehicle. Surely, the culprit would know I'd have given copies to the authorities. If they knew anything about me, they'd know I wasn't a clueless idiot.

Brad arrived first. I pushed to my feet, and he wrapped me in a hug. "You okay?"

"I'm fine. It doesn't look as if anything was taken. Whoever did this was hunting for the papers. Probably the same person who trashed Irma's place." Which made no sense. Who was this Bill?

McIlroy arrived with Rickson instead of Prentiss. I heaved a sigh of relief at not having to deal with the man who was quickly becoming my nemesis. I told him the same thing I'd told Brad and watched as the two officers entered my vandalized store.

By now, a crowd gathered in front of the gym, all attention on Tail Waggin'. "You okay?" Evans, the gym owner asked. "Shar is in the showers. Want me to send someone for her?"

I shook my head. She'd be out soon enough.

Mrs. Murdock parked next to Brad's car and rushed toward us. She peered at the broken front window of my store. "Let me give you the name of a guy who can install a security system."

"I can take care of that." Brad smiled down at her, then up at the cameras overlooking the parking lot and store entrances. "We might get lucky with that."

"Where is the information stored?" And why hadn't I noticed the cameras before? "When were they installed?"

"When I returned from my business trip. That's where I went. To consult with the security firm." He pulled out his phone and made a call, asking whoever was on the other end to send the footage to his email. "We can check it on your laptop—"

My laptop! I raced up the outside stairs and barged into my apartment.

McIlroy and Rickson both whirled, guns drawn.

"Did you see my laptop?"

"No." McIlroy shook his head and put his gun back in its holster. "I almost shot you."

"The thief took my laptop."

"Please tell me you didn't have the contact lists on there."

"No, they're in my car." I plopped on the sofa. "All my…Wait a minute." I raced back downstairs, locating my laptop in the drawer we locked our purses in. Normally, I left it upstairs, but today, I stuck it in there when I grabbed my bag, intending to retrieve it later. I put a hand to my pounding chest. All my business records were on there.

I thought McIlroy would blow his top when he found the laptop wasn't missing after all. "Woman, you are a thorn. A poisonous one." He waved Brad inside. "No sign of the person who broke in."

Brad took my laptop and logged into his email. "Security footage might tell us something."

I peered around him as someone in a dark hoodie took a baseball bat to my front window, then climbed through. I couldn't see much of what went on inside the store, but at least we knew mostly likely a man with an ordinary build was the suspect. "Our Bill, or someone hired to search for the papers?"

McIlroy shrugged. "We don't even get a glimpse of his face."

"That's an emblem of some kind," Shar said.

"I didn't hear you come up."

"Sneaky like a fox, that's me." She tapped the screen with her nail, enlarging it. "Oval, white with red letters. What local company has a logo like that?"

Brad enlarged the photo. "You've a good eye, Shar."

"You can barely make it out in the glow from the streetlight."

Brad copied the picture. "I'm sending it to your phone, Detective. Trinity, I'll have cameras installed inside your store tomorrow."

"What if the one who broke in is watching us." I motioned my head to the crowd gathered outside. "It wouldn't be hard to ditch a hoodie."

Rickson stepped onto the sidewalk. The rest of us followed.

Most of those watching were men. None wore a dark hoodie in the late summer evening. I glanced at the trash can on the corner of the sidewalk. Noting where I looked, Rickson headed to the can and pulled out the hoodie in question. The logo was for a local grocery store. Not only did employees wear them, but I'd seen them on a rack for sale. Another dead end.

"We'll send it to the lab," Rickson said, "but I

doubt we'll get anything off it."

McIlroy asked a few questions, but of course, no one had heard or seen anything. A strip mall with an active gym, a busy theater, and a number of shops with customers and no one saw someone take a baseball bat to my window? Either they were all blind or one of them was lying.

"Let me see that jacket." I snatched it out of Rickson's hands and let Sheba take a sniff. "Find him," I whispered, handing the hoodie back.

Sheba mingled among the crowd. When she approached a man who looked to be in his early twenties, the man's eyes widened. His gaze met mine before he whirled and dashed across the lot.

"Go, Sheba." Brad, the two officers, and I took off after the man.

My dog cornered the guy next to a truck jacked up on oversized tires. Growling low in her throat, she stood inches from him as if daring him to run again.

I called her off the frightened man, letting McIlroy take over. He quickly cuffed him and pushed him to a sitting position on the blacktop.

"Who are you?"

"I need a lawyer."

McIlroy pulled him back to his feet and felt for a wallet. Finding one in his back pocket, he flipped it open. "All right, Ryan Hollings, you'll get one."

"I ain't talkin'."

"Maybe my dog can make you talk, and I'm not the law. Who hired you?" I crossed my arms. "All it takes is one word from me, and she'll gnaw on your leg like it's a T-bone."

He paled under the streetlight. "Some woman gave me a hundred dollars to find some papers with a list of names. I didn't find anything, I swear."

"No, all you did was make a gigantic mess that you'll use that hundred dollars or more to pay for the damage you did." I fought the urge to deliver a swift kick. "Not to mention how much you scared my cats."

"One in the back howls like a banshee. Scared the bejesus out of me until I realized what it was."

I grinned. "His name is Prince." Maybe I could advertise him as a guard cat.

"Come on." McIlroy took Ryan by the arm and led him to the waiting squad car.

"Wanna bet Irma hired him?" Brad said.

"I'd bet on it. Which means, she hasn't left town." How could we draw her out? She obviously wasn't going to do her own dirty work, and there were plenty of punks willing to do her bidding for a price.

"Wanna stay with me tonight?" Brad glanced down at me.

"No. My cats are freaked out, and I have to straighten up my apartment. Shar and Heather will help in the store tomorrow. I'll be fine." I leaned back against him.

His chin rested on the top of my head. "I really wish you'd wait at least a year before getting involved in something like this again." His chest vibrated with a chuckle.

"All because I watched a Troublesome Twosome, and somebody killed their human." I sighed, realizing I still had the two of them with no interest from anyone to adopt them.

The squad car with McIlroy, Rickson, and Hollings pulled from the parking lot. The crowd started to disperse. Shar yoo-hooed from the store, waving a sheet of paper.

Brad and I hurried to join her.

"I don't know how McIlroy missed this, but that boy left you a message. I found it halfway under the counter."

"Overlooked." I took it from her and read. "Hand over all the names and let it be." I frowned. "Dumbest threat ever. It doesn't say who to turn the list over to, or what will happen if I don't."

"I didn't take Irma for a dummy," Shar said. "It looks like the corner is missing."

It did, not a large piece, though. "Neither did I." And that might make her the most dangerous person I'd come across yet.

# Chapter Eleven

Since the store was already in shambles, I let the Troublesome Twosome run loose while I cleaned up. You'd think I'd given Prince a Christmas gift as he chased papers around the room. Honey seemed content chewing on a beef-flavored bone. Sheba's brow creased as she watched the cat chase the papers.

Shar and Heather entered at the same time.

"I filled Heather in right away so she wouldn't be shocked." Shar eyed Honey and Prince. "You're feeling brave this morning."

"They can't be locked up twenty-four-seven." I handed her a box. "Start filing."

Heather sighed. "Good thing you have insurance. I'll call to have the front window replaced."

"Make sure it isn't someone who wants me dead." Last time the window needed replacing, the very person who came was the one who targeted me for death. I didn't care to repeat that experience.

"Anyone need a pick-me-up to clean this mess?" Brad shouldered open the door, his hands full of our morning drinks.

"Absolutely." I straightened a display rack and took the cardboard carrier from him, setting it on the counter. "You're the best pick-me-up." I smiled, waiting for his kiss.

He obliged, sending an electric current all the way to my toes. "You three will be at this for a while. Want me to hire some help?"

"No, we got it. The kennels are untouched, so the daycare can still run. Same with the grooming room. Any shoppers will have to step around the mess."

"I've been gone so often on business that we haven't had a date in a while. Let me take you to dinner tonight." His mouth crooked. "Somewhere nice and romantic."

"That sounds wonderful. Pick me up at six?"

"I can't wait." He gave me another kiss and headed across the parking lot to the theater. Brad could have his office anywhere but chose to do his work from there. Said he liked being surrounded by the stars of old. I assumed he meant the oil paintings of famous celebrities.

Prince streaked past me with something in his mouth. I chased him down, prying the paper from his mouth. My reward was a scratch on my hand. "Found the corner piece from the paper we found last night. All it says is park and 9:30."

Shar gasped. "That's the place and time of the meeting."

"I need to call McIlroy." I placed the call,

receiving a response he'd stop by on his way to the station.

"Gotta fix my hair." Shar made a dash for the bathroom.

"She's got it bad for a man who doesn't know she exists." Heather shook her head.

"Oh, he knows. He likes her as much as she does him but doesn't want to admit to it." I put the recent piece of paper with the one from last night in the cash register.

Shar joined us again, her hair sprayed and teased a few inches higher than before. Her lips sported a bright pink lipstick that matched the leggings she wore. Maybe the detective would be more willing to express his feelings if she toned her look down a little. I shrugged. Love would find a way.

As expected, his eyes widened at his first glimpse of her. Clearing his throat, McIlroy turned his attention to me. "You found something?"

I handed him the note. "I'm guessing it's tonight."

"I'll have someone make the drop."

"No way," Shar said. "You know the person who wrote that note is expecting Trinity alone. That's the way it always happens in every movie I've watched. She has to go alone."

"This isn't the movies, Shar." He frowned. "You of all people should know how dangerous it is to get mixed up in something like this. Haven't you been chased enough times lately?"

"Shar's right." I squared my shoulders. "Brad is taking me out to dinner tonight. We can plan to be at the park at that time. We'll stroll along the edge of the lake, and I'll carry a folder. I can make extra copies easy enough. Have an officer hide somewhere out of sight, but just one. Too many, and we'll spook Irma off."

"If she's the one who wrote that."

"Who else? The boy you arrested last night said a woman hired him."

"Fine, but I'm doing this against my better judgment. Where is Armstrong?"

"In his office."

McIlroy shot another glance at Shar, then marched across the parking lot.

"He is so fine." Shar heaved a sigh, fanning her face with her hand.

"Let's get back to work. I have a big night ahead of me."

Again, my store was full of people wanting to know all the details of the break-in. Even the man who came to replace the window had one ear glued to the gossip, which meant the window wasn't finished until after five. I left Heather to lock up and raced upstairs to prepare for my dinner date.

I'd just put my hair up when Brad arrived. "I'll be right out." Since he had a key, he could let himself in and be entertained by my fur babies while I finished getting ready.

"Sorry. The window guy took longer than expected." I smiled. Brad looked fabulous in black slacks, a royal blue button-up shirt, and tie. I smoothed my hands down the red dress I wore, knowing I looked my best.

"Still the prettiest gal I've ever seen." Brad

nuzzled my neck. "Smells good, too."

"Did McIlroy tell you about our after-dinner plans."

His expression grew serious. "Yes, and I'm not crazy about the idea, but we might get lucky and catch the person responsible for the vandalism."

I grabbed the bag containing my gun and the folder, then linked my arm with his and let him lead me to his car. A thrill traveled through me at the luxury of his Mercedes just as it had the first time I rode with him. Maybe I did want some of the finer things in my life after all. Life didn't have to be long work hours or struggling to make an extra dollar as my parents had done all their lives until retirement. I ran my hand over the soft leather seat. Why not step back and enjoy life once in a while?

At the restaurant, I ordered a filet with a blue cheese crust. We kept conversation away from the meeting at 9:30. I doubted anyone would show. Most likely, it would be Officer Rickson hiding in the bushes, and the young cop wasn't exactly subtle.

"What's been keeping you busy in your office every day?" I asked.

"New investments mostly. I'm thinking of replicating Waterfall Mall in other towns this size. There are more abandoned lots and buildings than there should be. Buying them and renovating will provide jobs. This state has a lot of people living at the poverty level."

"I like how your heart is always for someone else."

"No, sweetheart, you're the only one with a claim to my heart." His gaze warmed. "I do care about people, but you will always be my number one. Even over my businesses."

I sipped my water, my gaze locking with his. How had I gotten so lucky?

We lingered at the restaurant until eight. After that, we sat in the car wondering what to do until nine-thirty.

"We could get an ice cream," Brad said.

"I'm stuffed. We could hang out at the lake."

"What if the person we're meeting with sees us and tries to do the meeting early?"

"Hmm." Then, we'd have no backup. "I brought my gun."

He laughed. "So did I. Where do you intend to hide yours in that dress? Do you plan on carrying that oversized bag while we take our stroll?"

Good point. "I guess you'll be the only one packing."

He pulled me close for a kiss. "Let's hope it's enough."

We decided to head back to my place and get Sheba. Brad might be the only one with a gun, but my dog was a great alarm system. I changed into something more comfortable—black leggings and a flowing tunic—then joined Brad in his car where he'd changed from his dress shirt into a polo.

"I like you in that red dress, but seeing the shape of your legs is nice, too," he said as I slid into the passenger seat after putting Sheba in the back.

"I like the shape of you, too." My face heated. "Enough with the sweet talk. You'll distract me."

Laughing, he turned the car in the direction of the lake. "Wouldn't want do that."

He parked away from the few cars there. It might be late summer, but the nights had started to cool a bit, sending most people home by dark.

Was Irma here, or had she sent another hired person in her place? Did one of the few vehicles there belong to him or her?

I took a shaky breath and exited the car. With Sheba following obediently at my heels, I entwined my fingers with Brad's. "I'm ready."

"We'll be fine. I don't think anyone wants to kill you this time."

"Yet." The closer I got to solving this, the more dangerous things would become. "Good grief. Rickson is out of hiding." I spotted him pretending to feed the ducks. He wasn't in uniform, but anyone who lived in Waterfall would know he was a police officer.

"Don't go up to him." Brad held me at his side. "He's simply an off-duty officer. Let's move away from him."

We'd almost gone halfway around the lake when Sheba stopped and stared into a thick stand of trees. "Steady, girl." I put my hand on her head. "Who's there?"

"Drop the papers and move away." A man's voice came from the darkness.

"They'll blow away."

"Don't play stupid."

I glanced up at Brad. His brow lowered and his eyes narrowed. "Put the folder under a rock."

"I want to see who it is," I hissed.

"Hurry up," the man said. "I don't want you attracting the attention of that cop. I have a gun."

Why did people insist on stating they had a gun? Wasn't it better to keep that fact secret? I removed the folder from my bag and set it off the path opposite the hidden man. Let him have to venture out. I set a rock on top to keep the folder in place. "There you go." I called to Sheba, took Brad's hand, and headed back to the parking lot.

We hadn't gone far before Rickson sprinted past us.

I turned as a man emerged from the trees.

"Stop! Police." Rickson brandished his gun.

The man grabbed the folder and glanced our way. My gaze met that of Irma's son seconds before he darted back into the trees.

"I have a question about the weirdness of this. Irma has to know I'm smart enough to have given the list to the police and kept copies for myself. So, why would she risk her son to gain possession of them?"

Brad stared after Rickson. "Maybe she wants to know exactly who is on that list and who might cause trouble for her. Then, she can stop them before they expose her whereabouts."

Scary thought.

## Chapter Twelve

"Again, you had fun while I stayed home and watched late night television." Shar's lower lip protruded.

"I'll make sure to take you on my next date." I rolled my eyes and laughed. "At least we now know Irma's son is also involved in her scam." My chin rested on my hand. "Where could she possibly be hiding?"

Shar snapped her fingers. "Her son is dating Sally from the hair salon. What if Irma is staying with her?"

"Don't you think the police would have asked already?"

"Of course, but she might have lied to them. Maybe she'll talk to us." Shar grabbed the phone and asked for Sally, then hung up. "She's off today."

I grabbed my purse. "Tell me you know where she lives."

"I do." She grinned and glanced at Heather.

"Yeah, I know. Mind the store. I'm expecting a big raise one of these days," Heather said.

"You'll get one." I dashed outside, Sheba on my heels.

Shar barely spared her a glance as we climbed into the Thunderbird. "Irma lives in a duplex not too far away. I've seen her walking to work many times."

"You know what happens when we show up at someone's house unannounced, right?" I gripped the dashboard as she took a corner too fast.

"Yeah. We find a dead body."

Please, God, not this time. I stared out the front windshield for a moment when Shar parked in front of a cute duplex with white siding and dark green shutters. "It doesn't look like anyone's home."

"I'll pick the lock. Maybe we'll find a clue."

"What?"

"Oh, hush. It isn't like it's the first time." She pulled her little box of tools from the glove compartment. "Come on, Beast. You can alert us if someone comes." Shar gagged as Sheba swiped her tongue across her cheek. "I hate dog slobber."

"Sheba likes you." I exited the car and let my dog out. "Hurry up, before someone sees you."

"I'll have this door open in…" She bent over the lock. "One, two—" A loud click signaled her success.

My eyes widened as we entered. "We've stepped into the eighties." A white vinyl sofa bedecked with pink and blue pillows in a variety of patterns. A few plants hung over the front window, their long arms wrapped around the poufed curtain.

"I can't imagine Irma staying here."

"Looks like a teenage girl's bedroom." Shar opened a glass candy dish. "Spare key. No candy. Drat."

While she checked the front of the apartment, I headed down a short hall with a closet at the end. To my right, a bedroom. To my left, a bathroom. "Unless Irma is sharing a bed with Sally, she isn't staying here."

Something thumped on the other side of the wall, freezing me in my tracks. When it didn't sound again, I opened the bedroom closet. Only a few dresses and blouses. The dresser revealed leggings, tee shirts, spaghetti straps, and shorts. Definitely nothing to point to Irma.

The thump again. A muffled shout. Sheba, fur raised, stared at the wall.

Holding my breath, I pressed my ear to the wall. I couldn't make out what was being said, only that the voices were those of a man and a woman. A lovers' spat? A cry of alarm sent me hurtling to the front room.

"Something is happening next door." I grabbed an Avon book from the coffee table. "I'm heading over." A door slammed in the other duplex, and I froze in place.

Shar peered out the window. "A man just jumped into a jeep."

An engine roared, then the squeal of tires.

"We need to check on whoever is left." I set the book back. Pretending to sell Avon wouldn't have worked longer than a second, but it was the first thing I thought of.

"Okay, but if I get killed, I'm coming back to haunt you." Shar gripped my arm.

"We've been in worse spots."

"Looking for a suspect, not a recently murdered victim."

I shook her off. "We don't know that's what happened. It could simply be a marital argument."

"There's nothing simple about being around you."

After checking to make sure the cost was clear, we headed next door. The door hung ajar a couple of inches. "Hello?" I pushed it open the rest of the way. "Do you need help?"

No one answered. I stepped inside and headed for the back room next to the bedroom I'd been in. A woman's legs stuck out from the other side of the bed. I hurried to see Irma, eyes staring lifeless at the ceiling, a silk scarf wrapped around her neck. I fell to my knees and felt for a pulse. "Call McIlroy. She's dead."

If we'd been a couple of minutes earlier, we might have prevented her death. I pushed to my feet. The room definitely showed signs of the struggle I'd heard. A hole in the wall signified the thump. Blankets pooled over the furniture. Toiletries littered the floor, knocked off the dresser.

"If Irma is dead, then who is Bill?" Shar asked from the doorway.

"I think she's Bill. Whoever killed her wanted her silenced. Maybe it's about the watch scam. Or maybe it's about something more."

"Right. Maybe someone she scammed offed her."

"It's a good theory." We really needed to dig deeper in that contact list.

We both jumped and emitted squeaks when McIlroy and Prentiss entered the room. "A little warning, please," I said, putting my hand to my racing heart.

"Another body, Miss Ashford?" Prentiss raised a brow.

"We were next door when I heard a fight and a cry. A man sped away in a blue jeep. We came and found Irma dead." I'd gotten so used to telling details, I knew how to say them in the fewest words possible.

"Did you happen to catch the license plate number?" McIlroy checked Irma for a pulse.

"No, sorry. I was too focused on checking on whoever had been hurt." Killed, in this case. I lowered my voice. "Whoever killed Irma has to be on that contact list."

"Or her son," Prentiss said.

I shook my head. "I've seen her son. The man who ran out of here was not him. This man was stockier, maybe around forty-five, salt and pepper hair. I didn't see his face."

He crossed his arms. "How did you get in?"

"The door was unlocked and open." I matched his stance.

"The other duplex."

"We went to visit Sally." Shar smiled. "She wasn't home. Since we're friends, we let ourselves in. No crime in that." She slid her lock-picking tools into her back pocket. "Why are you always looking for us to be doing something we shouldn't?"

"Because you usually are."

"Back to the murder, please." McIlroy pulled a notepad from his pocket. "Find anything next door?"

He knew exactly what we'd been doing there. "Nothing. Clean as a whistle. Sally is a neat person. If I hadn't heard what went on next door, we'd have left none the wiser."

He bit the inside of his cheek. "I suppose you haven't had a chance to snoop around here."

"No." I glanced at Irma. "We thought at first she might be living with Sally. Didn't consider she might live next door."

"She owns the duplex," McIlroy said. "Last time we were here, there was no sign of her or her son."

"She owned more than two properties?"

"Five actually. Renters in all but this one and the larger house."

Hard to believe she'd gone from her lovely Victorian to this tiny duplex, but desperate people did desperate things. I glanced around the room noting a suitcase in the corner. It didn't appear as if she expected to stay long.

"You two can head home." McIlroy patted Sheba's head. "Nothing more you can do here."

"Come, girl." I slapped my leg. Outside, I turned to Shar. "We need to find that jeep. We find it, and we find the person behind all this."

"Right. Irma's scam got her killed. We need to find out who lost the most money because of her."

I still thought Irma responsible for Alice's death, but I could be wrong. It made sense that

Alice confronted her, she killed Alice, then someone else became angry enough to kill Irma. Most likely in a fit of rage rather than premeditation. The mental diagram in my head was spreading out. Alice and Irma, then Irma and the nursing home... "Hold on. The man who visited Serenity Falls was not Willy."

"The man we saw here?"

"Irma had a partner!" I lifted my hand for a high-five. "That's who we saw today. I'd bet Sheba's pink collar he also killed Alice. We need to find Willy and warn him. He could be next."

We returned to the store. Heather waved us to hurry, then locked the store door behind us.

"We're still open." I frowned.

"Shh. Sally and Willy are hiding in the storeroom. I didn't think you'd want to be interrupted while you talked to them."

"You're right. I'll rush them upstairs, then you can reopen the store."

"Want me to call the detective?"

"Not yet. Shar, come with me. Sheba, come." I opened the storeroom door. "Upstairs. Quickly."

The two young people thundered up the stairs to my apartment. I locked the door behind us. "Talk."

"Is my mother okay?" Willy fell onto the sofa. "A man came to the duplex. I saw him out the window of Sally's place. Mom called me on my cell and said to run. That you would hide us."

Why me? The woman had to know I'd turn him over to the authorities. Not to mention how his being here increased the danger to me and Shar. "Do you know who he is?"

"No." He bent, dangling his hands between his knees. "She's dead, isn't she?"

"I'm afraid so. We need to know everything. What is so important about that list?" I sat in a chair across from him.

Shar stood next to the front door, peering through the blinds over the small window. "All clear out front, but I don't like Heather being left in the store alone. What if these two were seen coming here?"

"I agree. Call McIlroy right now."

"No." Willy jumped to his feet.

"You'll be safe in protective custody. Now, what. about. the. list?"

"Mom said Alice had been contacting everyone my mother swindled. Alice said she was going to turn the list over to the police."

"Which I already did."

He nodded. "She figured as much, but she wanted to know exactly who was in Alice's contacts. By doing that, she'd find out why Alice was killed and whether my mother's partner killed her." He held up a hand to stop my questions. "I don't know who her partner is."

I'd suggest McIlroy send a sketch artist over to Serenity Falls. If we had a picture, we could tell whether it was the man who killed Irma and then, if we were lucky, get a positive ID.

Before McIlroy arrived, Willy grabbed Sally and dashed out the front door.

"You'll get yourself killed, you fool." Shar tried to block their way, only to find herself knocked on her backside.

"I'd rather die out here than in prison," he said clamoring down the stairs behind Sally.

Seconds later, they roared away in an older model Ford truck. I shook my head. "They won't make it out there for long. Whoever killed Irma will be actively looking for them."

"Their only hope is the police find them first."

"Let's join Heather before our mystery man shows up. Bring the beast. Four are better than one."

# Chapter Thirteen

I made sure to grab my gun before following Shar and Sheba to the store. Barely lunchtime and danger loomed on the horizon. Not even noon and we'd found a dead body and failed to protect two fleeing, potential victims. Definitely not a mundane day in Waterfall but one becoming ordinary to me.

"Are we expecting someone else?" Heather's attention had pivoted from watering the puppies for sale to us, now overfilling their dish. "Oh." She dashed to the storeroom and fetched a towel.

"Since Irma's son came here, it's possible the man who killed her will too." I set my gun on the backside of the counter where it couldn't be seen by anyone entering the store.

"I told you after being chased through the woods by an angry man with a gun that I no longer want your adventurous life." Heather wiped up the water from the cage. "I'm going home. The two of you—" she wagged her finger between us, "are the real Troublesome Twosome." She tossed the towel on the table, gathered her things, and marched out the door.

"And now there are three." Shar sagged into a chair.

"I don't blame her." I played with Sheba's ears. "I'm hoping the guy doesn't show. If he's smart, he'll run as fast in the opposite direction as he can. Did you call McIlroy?"

"No. Willy said not to."

I sighed. "The police need to be hunting for him and Sally." I gave Sheba another pat and retrieved my phone. The call went to voicemail, so I left a message. I started to call Brad, but his Mercedes wasn't parked in front of the theater. Which meant he was out on business. I wouldn't disturb him unless I needed to.

I rejoined Shar at the table, hoping for some looky-loos to come in, anyone to break the monotony of not knowing whether Mystery Man would show up. My fingers drummed as I stared through the front window.

"Don't you have work to do?" Shar asked.

"Yep."

"Me, too." She huffed. "I should be working on the van. Calls have started coming in from the advertisement." She remained seated. "Do you sometimes wonder whether we're all right in the head?"

"Because of getting involved in murder? All the time." I grinned.

She laughed. "It sure is exciting though, isn't it?"

"Yep, but I'm thinking we need to find another

form of excitement." Wasn't my store and Brad enough to fill my life with purpose? Did I need to find justice for every victim in Waterfall? Who would make sure justice was served if I became the victim? Answer—Brad would move mountains to find out who harmed me.

I stood as McIlroy entered the store dressed in street clothes. "You're off today?"

"I do take time off on occasion." His brow lowered. "But, I was passing by so thought I'd come get clarification on your message."

"You look better in jeans that your dress pants," Shar said, fluttering her eyelashes. "Too bad you can't always wear denim. Although I do miss seeing a gun on your hip."

Red blotches appeared on his neck. He cleared his throat. "Well?"

"Willy Grable came here. Said his mother has a business partner. She wanted the list because she was convinced Alice's killer is on it. Alice was asking a lot of questions about the watch scam." I bit my bottom lip, knowing he wouldn't be happy about the next part. "I mentioned calling you, and Willy and his girlfriend, Sally, ran off. She works at the salon across the parking lot."

"I doubt she does anymore," Shar pointed out, studying her nails. "First place a killer will look is your home. Second is your place of work. Sally might not have all her rocks polished, but I doubt she'll head to either of those places."

McIlroy's lips twitched. Was he fighting a smile? Maybe there was date in their near future.

A noise thumped upstairs.

Sheba stared up the stairs, her hair bristling.

I grabbed my gun from behind the counter and handed it to the detective. This time, I might be willing to let him take the lead, but I'd be right behind him.

"Stay here," he ordered. His gym shoes made very little noise as he headed up.

I glanced back at Shar, who waved her hands for me to follow him. She'd be right on my heels. "Go, Sheba."

The dog padded past McIlroy and into the apartment.

"What in tarnation?" McIlroy slipped my gun in the back of his waistband. "Trinity, call off your dog."

I peered into my apartment to see Willy peeking out from the closet. "I thought you were gone."

"That's what I wanted you to think." He eyed Sheba. "Since your store doesn't close until five, I thought we could hide in here until then, but that black and white cat knocked a glass off the coffee table."

"Cats do that." Thankfully, the soda he filched from my fridge landed on wood and not carpet. I rushed to clean it up, leaving Willy and Sally, who followed him from the closet, to deal with the detective.

"Sit." McIlroy pointed at the sofa.

"We didn't know where else to go." Willy plopped to a sitting position. "We ran across the parking lot in case the man who killed Mom was watching, then circled around. The door wasn't locked."

"I locked it this morning."

"We unlocked it earlier," Sally said. "So we could get back in."

"This was planned all along?" Clever. I didn't think the two of them had the brainpower between them to think that far ahead.

"Who is your mother's partner?" McIlroy asked.

"I don't know."

"Where can we find him?"

"No idea."

"I have one." I tapped the detective on the arm. "Why not send a sketch artist out to Serenity Falls? At least we'll know if Irma's killer is the same man who sold watches to the old folks."

"That's actually a good idea. You two come with me."

Willy shook his head. "Some of the people in jail bought my mom's watches."

"She was everywhere, wasn't she?" Shar crossed her arms. "I've heard of inmates ordering food from restaurants on occasion, but this is new."

"She has…connections."

"Of the criminal kind?" Shar arched a brow.

"We're getting off topic." McIlroy narrowed his eyes. "You'll be safer at the station."

"You don't know how long it will take you to catch this guy. I'm not going to sit in a holding cell for days or weeks." Willy shot to his feet. "We'll find a place."

"I have an idea." I didn't want to bother Brad, but he could pull strings I couldn't, so I took out my phone.

"Hey, Babe."

"Hey, yourself." I explained about Willy and Sally. "Do you think the apartment complex might have somewhere for them to stay? The security there is the best in town."

"I do own the place." He chuckled. "Have McIlroy bring them over. I'll meet them in the lobby."

"Thanks." I smiled and hung up, knowing I could always count on my man. Then I relayed his message. "I'd also like to be there with the sketch artist. Those people trust me."

McIlroy nodded. "Since it's my day off, I'll let you take these two to the apartments."

"The two of you will never have stayed in such luxury." Not wanting to leave Shar alone in case the store had an unwelcome visitor, I handed Willy the remote and told them to stay locked in my apartment until five o'clock. Then I texted Brad the time we'd meet him and saw the detective out. "Enjoy your time off."

"I will. Two days of fishing, but I'll have my phone on me."

Great. I'd most likely have to see Prentiss again. Rare was the day when I didn't have to speak to the police at some point.

At five o'clock on the dot, I locked everything up and led the two young people and Sheba to the alley where I parked my vehicle. "Inside and duck down, quick." I glanced around to see if anyone watched us. With the coast clear, I sped to the parking garage of Brad's apartment complex. "Stay close. No one can come inside the building without a garage pass or checking in with the doorman.

Other than jail, this is the safest place to hide."

Brad waited for us in the lobby as promised, his gaze warming as it landed on me. "Still neck deep, huh?"

"The flood never recedes." I grinned and linked my arm with his. "Lead on, kind sir."

"I've got them a small apartment on the fifth floor usually reserved for staff. We're short a maid so it's vacant." He eyed Willy and Sally. "Either of you want a job? It would give you something to do while you wait for things to settle down. I can use a maid and a man in the kitchen."

They glanced at each other, then nodded.

"Great. Let me show you where you're staying, then to your jobs." He handed them both a keycard. "I've already informed the doorman you're here, but I strongly suggest you do not leave this building."

Along with the two frightened young people, I followed Brad to the elevator, holding the door for Sheba who held back. "Come on. Since when have you been afraid of these things?"

She cast me a soulful glance and stepped inside. Poor thing. Moving floors were probably strange to an animal. When the doors whooshed open, she was the first one out.

The apartment Willy and Sally would be staying in was modern and clean with sleek lines. Black, gray, and white with a few navy-blue pillows thrown in for a slight contrast. The place definitely needed a personal touch but would suffice.

Brad handed Willy a business card. "I'm in the penthouse. Call me if you need anything or alert the concierge downstairs. Here are some meal tickets. I'll give you an advance on your paycheck so you can buy some clothes and food items. Have them delivered. Do not go out."

"Yes, sir. Can we have someone go to Sally's and pick up some things? Then to my place for my clothes? I'd rather save the money if possible. Once this is over, I'm leaving this city." Willy lowered to the black sofa.

"I'll see that it's done. Let me introduce you to the people you'll be working with." He glanced at me. "Want to stay? I can have room service delivered upstairs."

"I'd love to." While he took the two downstairs, Sheba and I went up to the penthouse.

While I enjoyed the coziness of my apartment, the luxury of the penthouse was nothing to stick my nose up at. I lingered in the doorway of Brad's room, remembering the sight of his father murdered in his bed. Thankfully, the bed and all other evidence of the violent death were gone.

I'd spent many a night under that roof in the guestroom but didn't want to live there permanently. My dream was to buy an old Victorian or one of those country houses with a wraparound porch and renovate it to its former glory. I moved to the window and stared ten floors down at the sidewalk, smiling. Maybe not a New York penthouse, but the building still towered over everything thing else in Waterfall.

From this height, I could even see the lake. Trees towered over the homes that made up Waterfall. To my left shopping centers and businesses were devoid of trees. The view present two completely different worlds.

Movement below caught my attention. The man who had run from Irma's duplex stared up at me. At least, I thought it was him. I jumped back. Who else would be interested in the penthouse? A few seconds later, he shoved his hands in his pockets and headed down the sidewalk.

## Chapter Fourteen

"Darling." My mother smiled at me as I opened the store.

"Mom? Dad?" I glanced from one to the other as they stood on the sidewalk.

"Are you going to let us in?" Dad kissed my cheek. "It's been a long flight."

"Oh, of course. I wasn't expecting you." I stepped back, anxious to see their reaction to what I'd accomplished.

Mom clapped her hands. "What a marvelous store. So much more than I imagined. Isn't it, Joe?"

"Yes, Lou, it is." He set a suitcase on the floor and headed to the puppies for sale. "What sweet creatures. But what is that noise?"

From the kennels came a familiar howling. "A cat whose owner died. I'm trying to sell it and the dog."

"Your mother and I are looking for a house. Maybe we can take them off your hands if they aren't sold by then."

"They're both menaces." I smiled. "Where are you staying now?"

"With you, of course." Mom smiled. "I hope you don't mind. It won't be for long."

"A house or an apartment?"

"Definitely a house."

There went my brilliant idea of them renting from Brad. "It's not a problem. Let me show you upstairs before I open for the day." I led them upstairs to my bedroom. "I can sleep on the sofa easy enough." Wonder what Brad would feel about them staying in his guestroom? "Once my employees arrive, I'll have to leave for a bit."

"Investigating?" Dad wiggled his eyebrows. "We've kept up on the news."

I laughed. "Introducing a sketch artist to some folks at the nursing home. Nothing as exciting as tracking down a killer."

"We'll be fine," Mom said. "Your dad and I have listings to look at. I'm sure we'll find our new home before the day's end."

"No rush. Maybe we can meet up for lunch." I gave them both a big hug, introduced them to my three fur babies, and told them about Shar and Heather. "You'll like them both. See you later."

By the time I returned downstairs, my friends had arrived. I told them of my parents' arrival and said to introduce themselves. "I'm off to Serenity Falls. Come, Sheba." I didn't want my puppies to distract my older friends this time. They needed to focus on the phantom named Bill.

I arrived at the nursing home in time for breakfast. Before I slid out of my car, my cell phone rang. "Hello, Valerie."

"Any closer to finding the missing jewelry? Bill?"

Straight to the point. "We are getting closer to Bill. It seems he was your mother's friend and Irma's business partner. Irma is dead. We're trying to determine if this Bill is the man who killed her. Unfortunately, no sign of the necklace or tiara yet. Hopefully, we'll locate those when we identify Bill."

"No luck with the contact list?"

"The police are working through it. But I'm trying to find Bill. I do believe he's on that list." I winced, realizing I still hadn't had the time to study the names there yet.

"All right. Sorry I've been MIA, but taking care of mother's affairs has consumed all my time. She had a lot of debt."

"Enough debt to cause her to be involved in a scam?"

"Are you suggesting she might have bought into Irma's scheme, then wanted out?"

"It's a possibility."

"Good. Work that angle." Click.

With a sigh, I exited the car and entered the nursing home. Sheba knew exactly where to go, her nose leading her to the dining room.

A man appearing ill at ease quickly approached me. "Please say you're Trinity Ashford."

"I am. Sketch artist?"

He nodded. "Larry Johnson. These people won't talk to me."

"Sure they will." I led him to the three I always

spent time with. "Margie, Hank, and Frank, this is Mr. Johnson. We're hoping you'll cooperate with him in drawing a sketch of the infamous Bill."

"With your endorsement, sure." Hank motioned to an empty chair. "Caucasian. A real pale fella who doesn't spend much time in the sun."

"Shape of face?" Larry asked.

"Pudgy," Margie said. "Not fat, exactly, but soft. Oval, like an egg."

"Exactly," Frank added. "He had an egg head, except dark hair. Hung below his ears and slicked back like a shyster."

So far, he sounded exactly like the man at Irma's duplex. These three didn't miss anything.

"He had a high voice." Margie tapped the drawing pad.

"I can't draw his voice, ma'am." Larry kept drawing. "Nose? Eyes?"

"Kind of a flat nose but not too flat," she said. "Eyes were brown, no, yes. Light brown. Like fine whiskey. They really were the most attractive part of the man. A nice oval shape, too. Isn't that strange? Oval eyes in an oval face?"

Hank and Frank nodded like matching bobbleheads. "Built, though," Frank said. "Like he worked out a lot. His body definitely didn't match the softness of his face."

When Larry finished, he turned the sketch around. "This your guy?"

"That's him." Margie high-fived Hank. "You are a talented young man."

"He'd be on his way earlier if you three would have talked to him," I said.

"We don't trust many people after that shyster." Frank frowned at the drawing.

Outside, I thanked Larry for his patience. "They didn't mean to be rude."

"I understand. Those three ought to work surveillance. Their memories are amazing." He tucked the sketch pad under his arm and headed for a white compact car.

"Wait." I ran after him, Sheba bounding along with me. "Can I take a picture of that? I have someone I'd like to show it to."

"Sure." He set it on the hood of his car.

I snapped a photo, thanked him, and returned to my car. A visit to the gym was in order. Not to exercise but to show the photo. The gym next to Tail Waggin' was the only one in town. Unless Bill had a home gym or was willing to drive twenty miles, he'd have gone there.

After dropping Sheba off at Tail Waggin' and promising to tell Heather and Shar what I'd learned, I hurried next door to the gym. "Have you seen this man?" I showed the photo on my phone to the people behind the counter.

"Sure. William Knowlson. Comes in every other night at seven," A young man said.

"You aren't supposed to tell people about our members, dude." Another man shook his head.

"It's fine. I own the pet store next door. Tonight?" Excitement leaped inside me.

"I think so, yeah." He shot a sheepish glance at his coworker.

"Thank you." I rushed back to the store. "Anyone up for the gym tonight?"

Shar shook her head. "It has to be someone he won't recognize. Not me, not you, not Brad."

"Not me," Heather whined. "I have a child to take care of."

"I'll get my father to go." Dad would be more than happy to do a bit of spying for his little girl.

~

"Remember, don't act like you know me," I told him before he left. "I'll come in fifteen minutes after you go."

"My backup, huh?" He winked, dressed in baggy shorts and a faded tee-shirt. "I'm sure your mother would rather show you pictures of the house we're buying."

"I'll look at them later. Be careful."

"I'm there to observe, nothing more. If I see him, I'll let you know so you can call the police." A quick hug and he jogged down the stairs.

"Your father has never been sexier." Mom fanned herself with her hand.

"Ew. I have fifteen minutes. Show me the pictures."

"It's a lovely little house on five acres, so there's plenty of room for the dog and cat. Has a stream running through it." She flipped through her phone, showing me a cute house with blue shutters on an expansive lawn. "Three bedrooms, one-and-a-half baths. Just perfect for us."

"You got the travel bug out of you? It's adorable."

"We'll still take trips but more like regular vacations. Might buy a camper so we can really get away." She propped her slippered feet on the coffee table. "Now, go keep an eye on your father so he doesn't do anything foolishly brave."

"Okey doke." I thundered down the stairs, wincing when I thought about the rascally pets. Sure hoped my parents knew what they were doing adopting Honey and Prince. I started to send McIlroy a text regarding my plans for the evening, then remembered he was fishing. Did I really want to contact Prentiss? No. Not unless I had something worth telling him.

I stopped just inside the door and surveyed the cavernous room. Several people used the treadmills. More used varying strength equipment. I showed my membership card to the front desk and roamed among the machines as if I were looking for one in particular. When I spotted my father pumping iron, I turned my head so he wouldn't try to flag me down.

After circling the entire place with no sign of Bill, I hopped on a treadmill and put my earbuds in, one eye on the door to the men's restroom. I motioned for Dad to go in.

Replacing the weights, he then gave me a jaunty salute and headed for the men's room. Bill exited as Dad tried to enter. My Oscar-unworthy father pretended to stumble, crashing into the suspect. Both men fell to the floor with Dad somehow managing to tangle his legs with Bill's.

I could not believe what I was seeing. So much so, that I almost forgot to text Prentiss to tell him we had the suspect in sight and to hurry.

Too late. Bill glanced up and caught me eyeing him. He shoved Dad off and bolted for the door.

"Stop that man!" Thankfully, I'd clipped the piece of the treadmill that stopped the machine because I needed to jump off. Rather than roll and land backside up, I landed on my knees.

"I'll get him." Dad took off like a rocket—an older one but was no match for the more physically fit man.

I caught up with my panting father seconds before Prentiss stopped his squad car in front of the building. "That way." I forced the words from breathless lungs, trying to ignore the burning in my knees. I hadn't skinned them since I was a child.

"Sorry, sweetheart. I tried to hold him." Dad leaned against the wall.

"Yes, you did." I put my arm around him and led him home. "That police officer will soon come and read me the riot act, and I expect you to be quiet. He's new and not used to me yet."

"I won't stand back and let anyone browbeat my little girl." He stiffened.

"It doesn't mean anything."

We hobbled up the stairs and into the apartment. Brad sat on the sofa next to my mother as she showed him pictures in an old photo album.

"Mom, really?"

"This nice young man came looking for you. I told him you were out with your father, and he could keep me company."

Brad's smile faded. "What happened to your knees?"

"Why is your shirt untucked, Joe?" Mom's eyes widened.

"We've quite a story to tell." Dad sat next to

her. "I had a tussle with the suspect and lost."

"I fell off the treadmill in my effort to help Dad."

Brad helped me into a chair. "I'll get the medical kit and clean those scrapes." He returned a few minutes later and wiped my knees with antibacterial wipes.

I hissed. "I should have been more careful, but he was getting away. Well, he did get away."

"You should use mercurochrome," Mom said. "That's what I used when she was a child."

Brad shuddered with me. "I wouldn't put that on my enemy."

"Thank you." I patted his shoulder.

"Keeping it all in the family now, are we?" Prentiss darkened the open front door.

# Chapter Fifteen

I fell asleep that night, smiling at the way my mother had put Prentiss in his place. Father kept his mouth shut and let Mom shoot holes in the officer for not catching that Bill guy and leaving it up to her precious daughter to put herself in danger because the authorities were inept.

I woke still smiling and rolled off the sofa, sniffing the air and catching the delicious aroma of coffee. "Good morning." I wrapped my mother in a hug. "I'm so glad you're here."

"Me, too, sweetheart. Today, we'll sign the papers on our new home and empty our storage unit. It'll be nice to put down roots again near our baby." She cupped my face. "And I adore your Brad."

"Thanks, I do, too." I stepped back and accepted the mug she handed me. "He always brings me my mocha-flavored coffee in the mornings."

"You'll be fine. You need to be alert to catch that scoundrel."

Wired would be more like it. While we enjoyed our coffee, I filled her in on everything, starting with Alice's murder.

"I like her creativity in hiding her valuables," Mom said. "I'll have to remember that. Are you sure this Valerie is honest?"

"Why wouldn't she be?"

"Well," Mom set her mug on the table. "You said she had quite a pile of jewelry after her search, and how many people have tiaras these days? Where would a woman like this Alice have need to wear one? She might have been wealthy, but she wasn't royalty or a celebrity."

"Why would she lie?"

Mom shrugged. "That's what you need to find out? I know her mother was murdered, most likely by this Bill or Irma, but my gut tells me her daughter is withholding information."

"You feel that without having met her?" I narrowed my eyes over the rim of my cup, not sure why I defended Valerie. We weren't more than acquaintances. "She's paying me twenty-thousand to find those items."

"She won't have to pay you if you never locate them."

True. I sighed. "How do I find out the truth?"

"The truth always comes to light." Mom pushed away from the counter. "Best wake your father and get this day started."

"I claim the shower first." A glance at the clock told me I was running late.

When I stepped out of the restroom, Dad called, "They posted a picture of that man we're looking for. Watch your back today."

"You, too, Dad." I left the door open to the stairs connecting the store, so my traitorous fur babies could join me once my parents left for the day. The two cats seemed content to curl up next to my parents on the sofa and watch the morning news.

Shar tapped her foot waiting for me to unlock the door. "Forgot my key. I could have been killed by a sniper standing out here waiting on you."

"Sorry. Had coffee with my mother." Today, I intended to scrutinize that contact list. I doubted Knowlson used his real name, but maybe he wasn't as smart as I gave him credit for.

Leaving Shar to her grooming and Heather to stocking and feeding, I pulled the papers from my bag, freezing as Mom came down the stairs with a leash. She waved and headed for the kennels, returning a few minutes later with a very excited Honey. "We might as well get used to each other. I'm afraid the cat is quite upset."

Upset didn't come close to the amount of noise emanating from the kennels. "Can't you take him with you in the carrier?"

She shook her head. "They need to get used to time away from each other. He'll be fine, and he'll learn that his friend will return." With that, she strode out the door.

Dad followed a few minutes later, casting a worried glance in the direction of the howling. "Can cats be leash trained?"

"Yes."

He grabbed a leash off the rack. "Bill me."

Soon, sounds of a knockdown, drag-out fight drew the three of us women to the kennels. Dad had the leash on Prince who twisted, climbed, hissed, and practically folded himself in half trying to escape. "Get me a valium," Dad said.

"You can't give that to a cat." I grinned, unashamed at enjoying the scene in front of me. "Have you tried removing the leash?"

"Of course, I have. This devil doesn't know what he wants."

"For crying out loud, Joe." Mom joined us, a leash on Honey that would lead two animals. "He only wants his sister."

The moment Honey came into sight, Prince settled down, and Dad exchanged one leash for another. "This furball is spoiled."

"They just lost their human, dear." Mom scratched behind the cat's ears. "They'll get used to us soon enough and learn the rules of the house."

"Good luck with that." I widened my eyes and stifled my laugh. To my surprise, Prince, tail in the air, walked peacefully beside Honey. Maybe the two would be all right with my parents after all.

"At least *we'll* have a peaceful day." Shar returned to the grooming station.

I met Heather's amused gaze. "I doubt my parents will."

"Maybe your mother can work miracles."

As we returned to the front, I told Heather of my mother's question regarding Valerie. "What do you think?"

"It makes sense." Heather leaned on the counter as I took my seat behind it. "I don't think she's working with this Bill, because…well, she wouldn't have had to involve you. What if there isn't any more jewelry, and she simply wants you to find him? It might not be about a necklace or tiara at all."

"Find Knowlson and then what? She confronts him about killing her mother? They weren't that close."

"Grief hits everyone differently."

Could it be that simple? I drummed my fingers on the counter. The only way to know for sure was to find Knowlson, so I turned my attention back to the contact list.

David, our delivery guy, pushed open the door and entered with a dolly full of boxes. He grinned at Heather, his teeth flashing against his mocha skin. "See you at six?"

She blushed and nodded. "Everything is ready?"

"It's about time," I muttered. My friend deserved a good man, and David was one of the best.

They whispered together, his head against hers, then Heather signed for the delivery. When he left, she turned to me. "I've invited him to dinner to meet Robbie."

"Yay." I clapped. "I want to hear all the details tomorrow."

"There won't be any. It's spaghetti and a family-friendly movie, that's all." She still smiled as she cut into the boxes, pulling out packages of pet treats.

A couple of minutes later, Brad entered. "Sorry, I'm late." He grinned. "But your mystery man was at the coffee shop a few minutes before I was. I thought maybe I'd spot him in the parking lot, but I didn't."

"He knows we're looking for him. Why would he buy his coffee so close to us?"

He handed me my drink, then left Heather's and Shar's on the counter. "Maybe he's toying with the police."

"Or maybe there's something around here he's hunting for." The question was what? "Could he be interested in this list?"

"Maybe there's someone on there who knew something about him, like Alice did."

I nodded. "Irma and Alice were both killed because of this contact list. If we don't find out more about these people, someone else is going to die."

"Make sure it isn't you." He leaned over the counter and kissed me. "If you need my help tonight, I'll be there."

"I probably will."

"Then I'll bring enough Chinese for us and your parents."

"That sounds wonderful." After he left, I pored over the list until my eyes blurred. I had to be missing something right in front of me.

"Maybe you're going about it wrong." Heather set the treat bags in their spots on the shelf. "Is Knowlson on there?"

"No."

"He's using a different name."

"I realize that. What I'm trying to figure out is who he's targeting next."

"An older, single woman. Call them, pretending to be customer service and ask how they like their smart watch. Then, go from there."

"Great idea." I grabbed a pink highlighter from a pencil holder and highlighted all the women's names.

I hit pay dirt on my fourth call. Greta Schmidt.

"Oh, yes, I have a lot to say to customer service." She made a noise in her throat that was anything but flattering. "The watch barely told time, made my wrist stink, and left a red outline on my skin. The watch was black!"

"I'm sorry to hear that. Have you heard back from your salesman?"

"He took my money and split."

"Your watch was sold to you by Bill, correct?"

"Yes. If I ever see him again, I'll throttle him. It doesn't matter that I'm seventy-years-old."

"Have you reported him to the authorities?"

"That's a strange question for customer service to ask. What kind of company is this?"

Now, how to get myself out of the hole I'd just dig. "My apologies. This isn't customer service. I'm investigating this scam, talking to those involved."

"How many did he swindle?"

"A lot, ma'am. The police are actively searching for him. Anything you can tell me will help us save other people from this same horrible experience." I pulled a sheet of paper from the printer and chose my favorite pencil to take notes.

"I've been getting strange phone calls."

I stiffened. "What kind of calls?"

"Where they listen and hang up or ask for

someone who doesn't live here."

What is Knowlson trying to do? "No other questions asked? Do you live alone?"

"I have a woman who comes in for a couple of hours a day, but she hasn't been here in a while."

"May I have her name?"

"I only knew her as Dorothy."

Is Dorothy the same as Alice or Irma or someone we haven't met yet? "Did you hire her through an agency?"

"Classifieds. I have the paper if you want to come see for yourself."

"I'd love to." She gave me her address, and I promised to be there in fifteen minutes. "I'll be back." After shoving the list into my bag, I called for Sheba and raced to my car. This wasn't the first time clues were hidden in the classifieds. Last time, I'd received personal threats on a daily basis.

Seeing I only had a quarter tank of gas, I drove to the nearest gas station. While I filled up my tank, a dark SUV pulled up in front of the building. No one got out to purchase anything from inside. The hair on my arms stood at attention. I'd learned from prior experiences to listen to my body's warning signals. Should I confront or flee? If I fled to Mrs. Schmidt's house, the SUV would follow, putting the woman in more danger than she was already in. I chose common sense and drove to the police station.

As I exited the car and approached the station's front door, I glanced over my shoulder to see the SUV stop at the entrance to the lot. A baseball cap pulled low hid the driver's face, but I knew without a doubt it was Knowlson.

I memorized the license plate number and typed it into my phone.

After a few minutes of staring each other down, the driver backed up and sped away. I rushed into the building, spotted Prentiss, and turned around and left. I'd text the number to McIlroy. I returned to my car and waited for my racing heart to calm down before driving to Mrs. Schmidt's. Through the front windshield, I spotted Prentiss step outside. He lit up a cigarette and turned to watch as I backed from my spot.

## Chapter Sixteen

Mrs. Schmidt lived in an eight-unit apartment complex in the center of town. Her apartment was the second one on the bottom floor. I motioned for Sheba to come with me and knocked on the door.

A woman topping five feet with snow white hair inched the door open just enough to peer out. Her gaze dropped to Sheba whose tail thumped the ground, sending up a small cloud of dust. "Miss Ashford?"

"Yes. Mrs. Schmidt?" I smiled.

"The very one. Come in." She opened the door wide and rushed to the kitchen, returning with a damp rag, which she promptly used to wipe the dust from my dog's tail.

The small apartment, while clean, sported crocheted doilies and afghans in a vast array of colors, making the space warm and inviting. Watching her wipe down Sheba, I didn't think the dust would dare leave a speck.

"The newspaper is on the coffee table." She bustled back to the kitchen. When she returned, she kissed the top of Sheba's head. "Now, you won't make me sneeze. My, you are a big girl."

Smiling, I opened the paper to the classifieds. I did love it when people adored my fur babies. I found the circled advertisement and compared the phone number to those on the contact list.

"Did your caregiver come in the evening or morning?"

"It depended on the day. Why?"

"Was she young?"

"Yes, too young, actually. Tea?"

I nodded. The advertisement number matched that of Willy's girlfriend, Sally. I lowered myself on the sofa, its plastic covering crackling under me. There'd been no denying how frightened the young couple had been when they arrived at my apartment. Who was the liar here? Valerie, Sally and Willy, or someone I hadn't uncovered yet? I'd be asking the two young people some more questions that evening.

Mrs. Schmidt handed me a cup of tea in a porcelain cup which sat on a matching saucer. On the edge of the saucer was a lemon cookie. She tossed one to Sheba, then sat in a chair across from me. "Well?"

"Thank you." I didn't usually forget my manners.

"Not that. What did you find out?"

"Oh." My face heated. "Your caregiver may be the girlfriend of the son of a woman recently murdered. I don't think this girl, Sally, or Dorothy as you know her, is the killer, but she is definitely involved."

"Quite an elaborate scam, these watches." She peered at me over the rim of her cup.

"It's more than just the watches." It was partly about Alice's jewelry. Somebody was killing to get their hands on a lot of money.

"Are you a private investigator?"

I laughed. "No, I own a pet store and pet day care."

"Got any cats? I've been wanting to get me a couple. Give me something to do other than crochet all day."

"We do have a litter of kittens. Would you like male or female?"

"Bring me the two cutest males." She smiled. "Also, that white box contains the watch. Take it with you. Maybe you can give it to the police as evidence."

"I'll do that." I thanked her again for the tea and dessert, then excused myself and headed back to Tail Waggin'.

Mom and Dad pulled up right after I did.

"Got the keys." She dangled one in front of my face. "The storage unit will be emptied and delivered tomorrow. We'll be out of your hair."

"There's no rush. How did Honey and Prince behave?" I prayed it went well. The two needed a home.

"Let's just say I called and got the number of an animal trainer from your friend, Heather." Mom reached in and led the animals, still attached to the double leash, out of the car. "I have faith they'll be better behaved in time."

"I can still try to sell them to someone else."

"No, your father and I said we would take them. You wouldn't get rid of an unruly child, would you? Of course not. You'd teach them proper behavior." She marched into the store ahead of me and Dad.

"Your mother enjoys the challenge." He put an arm around my shoulders and listened as I told him about my morning. "Someone is controlling those two."

"At least someone was."

"Fear is a great motivator. Since Irma sold the watches along with this William guy, I'd say she had Sally masquerade as a caregiver."

"Why?" I frowned up at him. "None of the others had a caregiver."

"I bet Sally and Willy visited everyone on that list in some way in order to feel out the customer."

"Again, why?"

"To see who would be a problem. Cause trouble and get disposed of."

"I need to talk to Sally and Willy. Find out who they've visited and find a way to visit the others myself."

"That's my girl. You'll figure this out in no time." He held the door open for me and Sheba. "You be careful. Let me know if you want me to come with you. I'm retired and have all the time in the world to help you."

"Thanks, Dad." I leaned into him, then sat in my chair behind the counter. Work called. I had invoices to pay and emails to check. "Oh, Heather, pick out the two cutest males in that litter of kittens.

Mrs. Schmidt bought them."

"If she isn't too far out of the way, I can deliver them on my way home."

"That would be perfect."

Brad called, inviting me and my parents to supper at his place. I agreed, telling him I needed to talk to Sally and Willy at some point.

Mom's eyes widened as we stepped off the elevator on the penthouse floor. "What does Brad do?"

"He's in business." I grinned. I could have told them before that my boyfriend was wealthy, but I wanted my parents to like him for him. Not that they were shallow, but they always told me to find a rich man. "He owns this building and the strip mall where my store is located. Not to mention other properties around the state."

"Lucky girl. Handsome and rich."

Brad opened the door as we exited the elevator. "Welcome."

"My oh my." Mom glanced around the place. "Very modern."

"My father lived here before his death. I met Trinity and stayed." He leaned down and kissed me. "Come, make yourselves comfortable. That fat furball on the sofa is Moses."

"Need any help in the kitchen, or did you order from the restaurant?" I asked.

"I cooked." He wiggled his eyebrows. "Surf and turf, loaded baked potatoes, and a salad. It's all ready." He'd already set the table with fine china and crystal.

"I guess you're out to impress," I whispered.

"A little." He poured glasses of wine, then motioned for us to take our seats.

Mom filled us in on the trials of Honey and Prince. "That cat almost strangled Joe, jumping on his shoulder, walking across his chest, and twisting the leash around his neck. Poor Honey fought on the other end, keeping things tight." She patted Dad's shoulder. "I thought he was going to throw the poor thing out the window."

"I will if he doesn't start behaving." Dad raised his glass in a toast. "To good food and crazy animals."

"I can cheer to that." I clinked my glass against his, filled with joy along with fine food.

After we ate, I helped Brad clear the table and load the dishwasher. "Do you want to come with me to speak with Sally and Willy?"

"Why don't I have them come up for dessert? Soften them up with cheesecake?"

"That's a great idea."

An hour later, Willy and Sally, their eyes darting in all directions, entered the penthouse. "A party?" Sally asked.

"Just a get together," Brad said. "Thought y'all might be going stir crazy."

"A bit." Willy sat down. "I'm not used to watching TV all day."

Mom handed them each a slice of strawberry cheesecake. "Coffee?"

"Sure," Willy said. He glanced at me. "I can tell this is more than a social gathering."

"True. I want to know whose idea it was for Sally to pretend to be Dorothy." I crossed my arms.

"My mom's." His shoulders slumped. "I swear she didn't know the watches were bad. She said her partner swore by them, saying she'd stumbled upon a way to get rich. Then complaints started coming in. First from Alice, then others. Mom thought if we could visit those making the complaints, we might be able to stop Bill. Instead, she got herself killed."

"Why not tell us all this upfront?" I retrieved the contact list from my purse. "Did you discover anything?"

"Not really. Just a lot of upset people." He set his plate on the coffee table.

"Cross off the people you've visited and those who didn't buy a watch." I handed him the papers and a highlighter.

"You think somebody knows something?"

"No, I'm trying to keep other victims from being killed." Mostly true. Find Bill, stop the killings. Somebody on that list knows him, and he might be hunting for them as I was. I needed to find them first.

When Willy finished, fewer than ten names remained on the list. I was surprised to see Mr. Mills of the hardware store not crossed off. "Are you sure all of these people bought a watch?"

He nodded and pulled up a file on his phone. "Mom kept records of every single purchase."

"Let me see that." When he handed me the phone, I sent the file to my email.

"Son, you could have saved yourself a lot of grief by turning this and everything you know over to the authorities." Dad leaned on his knees, his gaze piercing. "If you're still hiding something, now is the time to spill it."

I knew that look, having received it many times as a teenager. If there was anything Willy hadn't said yet, Dad would pull it out of him. I sat on the sofa and waited. "There's more to this than watches, isn't there? Do you know Alice's daughter, Valerie? Anything about a necklace and a tiara?"

He shot a quick glance at Sally. "We've never met Valerie, but Mom didn't care for her. Said all she cared about was her mother's money."

I got the same impression. "Go on."

"I don't know anything about a necklace or a tiara for sure, only rumors that they were stolen. Mom thought Alice had sold them to pay for that big house of hers. Her husband left her in a lot of debt when he died, and she paid off some things."

Something Valerie might not know. "And?"

"That's it. Other than the fact Valerie came in and out of her mother's life, I got nothing."

"Valerie needed money?"

He shrugged. "Don't we all?"

"What happened to the money your mother made off the watches?" Brad asked, accepting a cup of coffee from my mother.

"My mother didn't keep me informed about her finances." He also took a cup from Mom. "I didn't think she had any left, though. Bill took her for all she had before he killed her. Why else would she be living in that duplex?"

"I heard them arguing once," Sally said softly. "They didn't know I was there. I'd lost the key to my duplex and used the restroom in Irma's. They were fighting over Valerie. Irma told Bill that the woman was on to them, and they'd both wind up in jail. Irma said his ruse of dating Valerie wouldn't work anymore."

"Why didn't you tell me this?" Willy sprang to his feet.

"I didn't want to get involved any further than we already were. People are dying." She covered her face with her hands and sobbed.

"Valerie is dating Bill?" All this time, she knew exactly where the man she wanted me to find was. I'd strangle her myself.

# Chapter Seventeen

After numerous tries to call Valerie, I gave up. The woman didn't want to speak with me. Somehow, she must have found out I was on to her. I shrugged. Oh, well. I'd made twenty-thousand instead of forty, but I wouldn't complain. Business was good, and my family and friends were close by.

"I'm driving to my first mobile appointment." Shar jingled a set of keys in front of my face. "I have an in-store appointment at three. I'll be back by then." She disappeared down the hall.

After days, weeks, of repainting and rearranging the van's interior to meet her needs, she was finally ready. Shar had fallen in love with the van when I'd purchased it but still had to spend more time and money to "get it just right."

"It'll be a lot quieter around here with her gone." Heather smiled around the rim of her coffee cup. "To think I used to resent you hiring her."

I laughed. "I was a bit uncertain myself, but I can't imagine this place without her now."

"She's also someone for you to get in trouble with."

"That's for sure." Since Heather erred on the side of caution because of her son, I'd be snooping alone if not for Shar. It wouldn't be near as much fun. "I'm going to the hardware store. Won't be gone long." Grabbing the watch Mrs. Schmidt had given me, I headed outside and turned left.

Mr. Mills' name hadn't been crossed off the list, Willy said he'd purchased a watch and not been visited yet. That left me to see how the man felt about his purchase.

"Good morning, Mr. Mills." Glancing around, I was pleased no other customers were in the store. I set the stupid watch on the counter. "Would you have a battery for this watch."

He eyed it as if he'd catch a virus if he touched it. "You can't replace the battery on that piece of garbage."

"I can't?" I put on my best disappointed look. "It's brand new and doesn't do anything except tell time. I mean, it looks cool, but—"

"It's a scam." He slapped the counter. "I can't believe you fell for it, too."

"What do you mean? Do you have one?"

"Yep." He opened a drawer behind the counter and tossed a watch identical to the one I'd brought. "If I ever find that Bill again, I'll…never mind. There's nothing we can do."

"Have you tried to find him? Because when I called the number on the card he left, it went to a woman's voicemail."

"Same here." His face darkened. "I'll never buy

anything from a salesman again. Anyway—" he replaced the watch in the drawer. "I'm sure the con artist is long gone from here by now."

"I just bought the watch yesterday."

"You're good at finding people. Find this man, so I can give him a piece of my mind."

"Have you ever seen him before?"

"The bar on 65. Heard he was a regular there. I went once but didn't see him. Decided nothing good could come from me confronting him. I'd probably end up in jail for assault."

"Okay, thanks." Mr. Mills didn't seem to know anything that would put him in danger, but he had given me a clue. Hopefully, Brad was in the mood for a visit to a dive bar later that night.

Back at the store, I called McIlroy, letting him know Willy and Sally were safely at the apartment complex and about the list. "I spoke to Mr. Mills, but he didn't have anything new to say other than this Knowlson likes the bar out on 65."

"Max's?"

"I guess. Brad and I will go there tonight and let you know if we see him."

"If you do see him, don't confront him. Call me, and I'll send someone."

"What if he starts to leave? He knows my face."

"Do. Not. Approach." Click.

It would be nice if he said goodbye once in a while. I stuck out my tongue at the phone. What did Shar see in him?

"You could wear a disguise," Heather said. "Put on a wig and dress differently. I doubt Knowlson will expect you, so if you go with your parents and

Brad, he probably won't look twice."

"That's a brilliant idea. I'm headed to the thrift store." The place I always went to when I needed something to wear.

Mrs. Murdoch didn't disappoint. She led me to a display of wigs in all shapes and colors. "What would you like to be? Blonde or a redhead?"

I ran my fingers through the strands of a long blond wig. "This one." I refused to think of how many people might have worn it before me. "Can I just borrow it? I'll never need to wear it again."

"Sure. I make a lot of money off wigs at Halloween. Now—" she stepped back and studied me. "You don't want to wear your usual leggings and tee-shirts. No jeans, either. You need something slutty to go with that wig."

"Uh—" I'd never pull it off.

"Here we go." She pulled a strapless dress off the rack. "It'll hit you mid-thigh, so if you don't want to show what God gave you, stay out of the wind."

"It looks like something a vampire would wear."

"Good. Go with that. Wear heavy eye makeup and bright red lipstick. Brad's eyes will pop out of his head."

I'm sure they would. I took the items with me, feeling dirty already.

~

"I bought a toupee at a yard sale," Dad said when I called them about joining Brad and me that evening. "It's pretty convincing, too. Since Knowlson hasn't seen your mother, she can wear whatever."

"Why did you buy a toupee at a yard sale?"

"Your mother dared me to." He laughed. "We'll be out front of the apartments at eight o'clock. Since this guy might know your car, it's best we drive."

I hung up and drove to Brad's. Shar would be upset when she found out about tonight's adventure, but I didn't need my crazy friend spoiling our disguises. She wasn't exactly the type to blend into the background. Not that I'd be much better in my vamp clothes.

Brad looked sexy in faded jeans, a tee shirt with a band logo on the front, and a tattered baseball cap. He carried his handgun in a holster on his hip. "Well, hello, country boy." I gave him a quick kiss. "It's going to take me a while to get ready, but I'll be out by the time my parents arrive."

When I stepped out of the bathroom, Brad's eyes did almost pop out of his head. "Who are you, and what did you do with my girlfriend?"

"Too much?"

His arm snaked around me and pulled me close. "I don't think I can afford you."

I slapped his chest. "Will anyone recognize me?"

"I wouldn't even know it was you if you weren't in my apartment."

"Don't kiss me. You'll ruin my lipstick." I smiled, caressing his face.

Mom's and Dad's reaction weren't as favorable.

"Go change right this instant." Mom pointed at the front doors of the building. "People will think Brad has hired a prostitute."

"Only if they recognize him." I slid into the back seat. "Relax. It's only a disguise. I'm not going to turn into this person." I tugged at the hem of the dress, trying to make it more modest. If I pulled the hem, the neckline slipped. It would be a never-ending battle not to expose myself. "I should have dressed like an old woman."

"I like this better." Brad kissed my shoulder. "I'll have to fight off a lot of men tonight."

"Good thing you're carrying a gun," Mom said. "Women who dress like my daughter will draw them like flies."

I rolled my eyes. "We're there to observe and alert McIlroy if we see Knowlson. Nothing else."

"No reason not to enjoy a night out," Dad said, pulling onto the highway. A few minutes later, he found an empty parking spot in front of a clapboard building with a huge neon sign that said Max's.

Several motorcycles were lined up along the front of the building, and country music blared from inside. Here goes nothing. I slid from the car, keeping my dress in place, and linked my arm with Brad's. I wanted to show right off that I was taken.

Still, heads turned, and a few whistles followed as we headed for an empty table. Once I was seated, I scanned the room for Knowlson. If he was coming, he hadn't arrived yet. I hoped this getup wasn't a waste of time.

A server dressed in tight jeans and a tee-shirt with the bar's logo approached our table. "What can I get you folks?"

"Two beers," Brad said. "Ladies?"

Mom and I ordered a glass of red wine each.

Since I wasn't a fan, I'd nurse mine as long as it took. I kept my eye on the front doors and ignored the curious glances sent our way. My face heated at some of the lecherous gazes. The muscle ticking in Brad's jaw told me he wasn't pleased either. But, I recognized a few people there from town. They didn't greet me by name which meant my disguise worked.

"How long are we going to stay?" Mom asked. "The music is too loud."

"At least a couple of hours." Dad stood and held out his hand. "Let's two-step. You won't mind the music as much."

"I need the ladies room." I followed them to the dance floor, then continued to the sign that said Gals. I took care of business and stared at myself in the mirror while I washed my hands. It really was difficult to recognize myself.

I'd just stepped out of the restroom when someone growled. I whirled and stared into the round face of Knowles.

"I've not seen you here before," he said, a leer on his face. "This joint needs more dolls like you."

Dolls? I rolled my eyes and rushed back to Brad. "He's here. In the corner." Since I had nowhere to keep my phone in the silly dress I wore, Brad texted McIlroy.

"He'll be here in one minute. Said he's parked down the road in case we spotted Knowlson."

Smart thinking. When the song ended and Mom and Dad returned, Brad paid our bill. We headed to the parking lot so we didn't tip Knowlson off. Let the police handle him. I wanted to hurry home and change as quickly as possible.

McIlroy and Prentiss had parked close by in an unmarked car. Both wore street clothes and strode right past us.

I cleared my throat. "He's at a table in the corner by the ladies restroom."

McIlroy almost swallowed his tongue. "What in tarnation are you wearing?"

"Best I've seen her look." Prentiss laughed. "Is that your side job?"

"Shut up." Dad's fists clenched. "She's undercover. Avert your eyes."

"Just go get Knowlson, so we can—" My mouth dropped open as the man they sought exited the bar and strolled behind the two officers as if he didn't have a care in the world. "He's getting away."

Knowlson hopped on a Harley and sped from the parking lot as McIlroy and Prentiss sprinted for their car. The man glanced back just as I removed my wig and shook out my hair. I couldn't see his face due to his helmet, but I'd given myself away.

Knowlson increased his speed, rocketing down the highway. McIlroy wouldn't catch him, and now the man knew with certainty that we knew his identity and were after him.

# Chapter Eighteen

"I have some big dogs on my list today," Shar said as she entered the store. "I could use your help."

After quickly going over today's to-do list, I told her I'd be delighted. "We'll have to figure out a way for you to do this alone, though. I can't take off work all the time."

"Pshaw." She waved a dismissive hand. "You're always off for one reason or another."

Was I? I did take off a lot in search of clues. "I apologize. It's so unthoughtful of me." I had a business to run. "I've taken advantage of my friends."

"I don't mind," Heather said. "Bringing justice to someone who died an untimely death is important. It's not all the time, just in spurts. We had a couple of months where you were here every day, all day."

True, but it didn't make me feel any better. I needed to keep my gumshoeing to the evening hours so my employees could take a day off once in a while. "When this is over, Heather, I'm giving you a week's paid vacation." I grabbed my bag.

"What would I do with a whole week?"

"Go on more dates with David." Which I had yet to ask her about. Another pang of guilt hit me. "How did dinner at your place go?"

"Pizza, a family movie, and he played cars with Robbie. It was perfect." She smiled. "We're going to do that every Friday night and see where it leads us."

"I'm happy for you." I grinned and motioned for Sheba, then followed Shar to the grooming van.

"I get a lot of honks in this thing." She climbed into the driver's seat. "Hard to miss this bright blue thing driving down the road."

"Good advertisement. Maybe someday it will pay enough to hire you an assistant."

She cut me a sideways glance. "What did you do last night?"

I swallowed hard. "Went to Max's with my parents and Brad."

"Dressed as a harlot?"

My mouth fell open. I snapped it shut. "How did you know?"

"Girl, it's all over town how hot you were. The men are talking about the new woman Brad was with. Since that man is head over heels for you, I knew it couldn't be anyone else."

"I received a tip that Knowlson went there a lot and couldn't risk him recognizing me. Except, he did. I thought he was gone and removed my wig in the parking lot."

"Uh-oh."

"Exactly. I'm sure he informed Valerie I was on to him."

"One or both will be coming for you."

"I don't plan on being alone anytime soon."

"That hasn't stopped the bad guys before. What about your apartment?"

"I have Sheba and a gun."

"The penthouse?"

I shook my head. "My mother would have a heart attack if I slept at Brad's, guestroom or not."

"You could stay with them." She pulled in front of a small home surrounded by a chain-link fence.

"I'm thinking about it." I climbed out of the van and opened the wide door on the side. "What kind of dog?"

"Newfoundland. Its owner said he hates baths." Shar headed for the house.

I pulled the hose and wand from the back of the van. If the dog didn't appreciate being hosed off, it would be safer to wash him on the driveway than fight to force him inside. Maybe Sheba would distract him long enough for us to finish the job.

Shar fought to drag the big galoot of a beauty toward the van. Thankfully, the giant boy wasn't aggressive. Instead, he planted all four feet and tugged against her. Until he saw Sheba. Then, he whipped the leash from Shar's hands and bounded toward me and my dog.

While the two introduced themselves in the way dogs do, I clipped the chain on the Newfoundland that would hold him still. "Sit, Sheba."

My obedient girl did just that, and I secured the

chain. "What's his name?"

"Zeus." Shar crossed her arms. "He's unruly."

"Seems to be doing okay now." The chain on him kept him from sitting. I stepped back so Shar could work, staying close to Sheba to keep her in place so Zeus would cooperate.

After dried and brushed, the dog was more than happy to return to his owner who whistled from the front porch. Shar followed to collect the payment while I put Sheba back in the van. "Good girl."

I glanced up to see a big truck idling at the end of the street. The truck itself wasn't what caught my attention. Our town was full of rednecks with jacked-up trucks. The fact it idled and the driver's attention was clearly on me was what had spiders skittering down my spine.

"What is it?" Shar asked as I closed the side door.

"The driver in that truck seems to be watching us."

"Maybe he's waiting on someone." Shar headed to the driver's side.

"Maybe." I couldn't shake the feeling the driver watched us. "Want to break for lunch?"

"You bet. Burgers? We can sit outside and not have to worry about Sheba."

"Perfect."

She parked behind the burger joint. We placed our orders and sat at the tables in front that faced the road. "I have a collie to groom after we eat. She won't be a handful like Zeus, just all that hair."

I laughed. "You should take Sheba when you have unruly animals. She'll help keep them in line."

Shaking her head, she accepted a basket with a burger and fries from a teenager on roller skates. "I'll think about it."

"Just kidding." I dipped a fry in ketchup. "I like her with me. You're the groomer. Figure it out."

"What are you going to do about Valerie?" She tilted her head. "Have you tried calling her?"

"This morning. No answer. I'm sure she'll find me."

"Here's my question." Shar took a sip of her soda. "She paid you to help her find her mother's jewelry, and she knew where it was all the time. Then, she said she'd pay you again to find a necklace and tiara that might not exist. We find out she's dating her mother's business partner." She took another drag on her straw. "What's her goal here? Why call and hire you?"

"Maybe she's lost something and thinks that with my nosing around, I'll find whatever that something is." Except all I'd done was find out the identity of Bill. I gasped. "Bill took whatever Valerie is looking for. She doesn't want him to know she suspects him, so she's playing along and having me do the snooping."

"Then why isn't she returning your calls?"

"That's what I'm trying to find out." I gathered my garbage and tossed it in the trash, then glanced up to see the same truck pass the burger joint parking lot. "Time to go." We were definitely being followed and not by the same truck that followed me to the police station. As we headed for the van, I texted McIlroy the description of the truck. I pressed send.

The van exploded.

Shar, Sheba, and I were hurtled backward.

I landed hard on my shoulder and lay there trying to catch my breath and stop my ears from ringing. I struggled to a sitting position. I couldn't see. I was blind! I touched my head, bringing my fingers away bloody. No, blinded by a head wound. Using the hem of my shirt, I wiped my eyes clean and looked for the other two.

Sheba struggled to all fours and padded toward me. I wrapped my arms around her neck. "You poor thing. Are you okay?" I snuggled against her until I realized Shar wasn't moving.

"Shar!" I crawled toward her and felt for a pulse. Her heart was still beating. I turned my cheek to her mouth. She wasn't breathing. "Someone call 911." I started CPR, my sight now blurred with tears. "Call Detective McIlroy at the police station."

"No need." He gently pushed me away and took over. "I was close, getting my own lunch. Somehow, I knew the explosion involved the two of you. Come on, darling. Breathe for me. Don't die on me, Sharon."

The ambulance sped into the parking lot, sirens blaring as Shar's eyes fluttered open. "You know my name? You called me darling." Her lips curled into a weak smile.

"Don't move. The paramedics are here." He cupped her cheek, then stood. "Trinity, you need that head looked at. In more ways than one."

No argument here. Not today. I swayed. He caught me before I hit the ground and lowered me to a sitting position.

"It had to have been the driver of the truck I texted you about. I saw him here."

"I didn't get it."

"Because the van blew up when I pressed send."

"They used your phone number to detonate the bomb?" He paced the area while a paramedic helped me onto a gurney.

"Call Brad and my parents, and please have Sheba checked out by a vet."

He waved that he'd heard me and ran to his car, taking my dog with him. With a glance at Shar being loaded into the ambulance, he pulled a roll of crime scene tape from his trunk.

I almost felt sorry for the driver of the truck if McIlroy found him. A smile erupted. He'd let his feelings for Shar slip. She'd never let up now.

On the way to the hospital, a paramedic tended to my head wound and the multiple abrasions on my arms and legs. I worried about my dog and my friend, trying to turn my head to see how Shar fared. Every time I did, the paramedic pulled my head back to face him. "How bad is it?"

"You'll need stitches, ma'am."

"Can I cover the scar with my hair?"

He nodded. "It's close to the hairline."

The ambulance stopped, and the paramedic opened the two back doors, grabbing one end of the gurney. The wheels hadn't hit the ground before Brad and my mother were by our side.

"Your father went to take your dog to the vet," Mom said, smoothing my hair back from the bandage. "How are you feeling?"

"Like I almost got blown up." I reached a hand

out to Brad.

"Ma'am, they can come in after the doctor sees you." The paramedic shot them an apologetic glance. "Please wait in the waiting room." I was rushed past them into the hospital.

Shar and I were wheeled into a curtained-off alcove big enough for both gurneys. A nurse took our vitals, then promised the doctor would be in soon.

"You okay?" I turned my head toward Shar.

"Did you hear what McIlroy said?" Shar grinned.

She seemed fine. "I did."

"I'm going to invite him to supper. Do you know his first name?"

"No. Do you remember what happened?"

She blinked a few times. "We had lunch and headed for the van. I guess I passed out. Oh, did the detective give me mouth-to-mouth?"

"He pressed on your chest mostly."

"That works, too."

"Listen to me. We were walking to the van. I went to send a text to McIlroy. When I pressed the send button, the van exploded."

"It's gone?"

"Yes." Tears stung my eyes.

"I worked so hard fixing it up."

"Insurance will replace the van. Shar, it was the driver of the truck we saw. I'm positive."

Her features hardened. "I hope McIlroy finds him before I do because he's bound by law, but I'm not." She started to get out of bed.

"Where are you going?"

"To find this bomber."

"No, you're not, ma'am." The doctor entered. "Both of you will be with us for the night for observation. You're in no condition to go anywhere."

She flopped back. "I'll sneak out when you're off duty."

The doctor sighed. "I'll make sure you have a guard at your door. We'll also keep you busy with x-rays and tests."

I choked back a laugh. Shar had met her match in this young doctor.

# Chapter Nineteen

**By the time** the doctor determined we had a concussion and multiple bruises and abrasions and were put in a regular room, exhaustion melded me to the mattress. I didn't think I could move if Knowlson stepped to the foot of my bed. The nurse handed me a cup of water and a pain pill, which I gratefully accepted. My eyes drifted closed as my family entered the room. I fell asleep to their murmurs.

I woke to the soft conversation of Shar and McIlroy from the bed on the other side of a striped curtain. I kept my eyes closed so they'd keep talking.

"Your name is Alex. That's a nice name," Shar said. "Why did it take me almost getting killed for you to show your feelings?"

"It took an explosion to blow away the hard shell I kept around my heart. After my wife's death, I couldn't believe I'd feel this way again."

I smiled, keeping my head turned. Something

good had come from the van's demise.

"Excuse me, you two. Trinity?" I opened my eyes as Brad entered the room and peered around the curtain. "Feeling better?"

"Much. Is it morning?"

He shook his head. "Midnight, actually. Your parents are home with Sheba. She's fine. A few bald patches from scraping across the parking lot, but her hair will grow back. No broken bones. She's a tough pup." He kissed the bandage on my forehead. "You, on the other hand, received seven stitches to that hard noggin of yours."

I groaned and raised the bed to a sitting level, glancing at McIlroy. "Guess you didn't find the truck?"

"Found the truck but no one inside," he said. "It had been reported stolen a couple of hours before. There's no question your phone number detonated the bomb."

"I brought you a new phone with a new number." Brad set it on the bedside table. "I also had the phone company transfer all your contacts and photos."

"Thank you." I squeezed his hand. "My bag?"

"Right here." He set it next to me. "Why?"

"I had a thought while I was sleeping." I pulled out my laptop. "If Alice did own a diamond necklace and tiara, there might be a photo of her during her socialite days. Wasn't she once in the news a lot, or did I dream that?"

"I remember a few things about her from when I was young," Shar said, raising her bed as McIlroy pulled back the curtain. "She was a sought-after gal when she was young. It's a good idea."

"Let me, sweetheart." Brad took the laptop, set it on the mattress, and started typing. "If I can't find anything, I know someone who can. You rest and let me look."

"I can have someone at the precinct search," McIlroy said. "Shar, you should rest, too."

I didn't need more encouragement than that. My eyes drifted closed. I didn't know how long I was out, but when I woke up, Brad was sleeping in a chair beside the bed, and the detective was gone.

When I shifted, trying to get comfortable, Brad woke and smiled. "I found her." He turned on the laptop and showed me a photo of a young Alice in a ball gown wearing a stunning necklace and tiara. "Her debutante ball."

"She was pretty. Who are those people with her?" I scanned the faces of other young girls.

"McIlroy is trying to find out where they are. Their names are listed here with hers. One of them is Irma."

I peered closer. "Let Shar see this. She might recognize some of the names." So, Valerie was right about the missing items at least. What if she wasn't out to harm me but stayed out of sight to keep herself safe? That didn't make sense. I rubbed my temples. She dated a killer. She had to be involved. "We need to find Valerie. She has to be in Waterfall somewhere. Find her, find Bill."

"If she is here, she could be an accomplice to murder." Brad frowned. "I hate that she roped you into this."

"I got greedy. Another twenty grand sounded

very good." I exhaled heavily.

"You had no idea what saying yes would entail," Shar said. "Don't beat yourself up. I lost a van."

"*I* lost the van. I'm the boss, remember?"

"Oh, right. I sometimes forget." Her hands fell at her sides. "Has anyone let Heather know we won't be in today?"

"I did," Brad said. "She sends her love and says not to worry about a thing. She'll reschedule any grooming Shar has for next week."

"What would I do without you?" I entwined my fingers with his.

"Probably be in veterinarian school."

"Nope. Because I wouldn't have had your brain helping me make better financial decisions." Strange how my dream changed. Wanting to be a vet used to consume me. Now, being a successful businesswoman made me happy. If I didn't get myself killed one day.

The doctor released Shar and me later that afternoon, making us promise to rest for another day or two. I'd try but didn't make any promises. Now, I sat on my sofa, both my cats curled up next to me, and watched my mother bustle around to prepare homemade chicken soup.

"I'm not really hungry, Mom."

"You'll eat if I put it in front of you."

I sighed and turned on the TV, idly flipping through channels. What I wanted to do was go out and look for the man who blew up my van. But, the pain pill barely kept the aches and pains at bay. I wouldn't be much good to anyone for a day or two.

Lying on my side, I gathered the cats closer and napped, waking when a cold wet nose pressed against my face. I smiled and wrapped my arms around Sheba. "How's my girl?"

A lick of her big tongue let me know she was fine. The next time I woke up, it was to the delicious aroma of soup and the wonderful sight of Brad, reclining in a chair. He and my father must have been talking about me because they had guilty expressions on their faces when I sat up. "What are you guys up to?" I frowned, then grimaced.

Brad leaped to his feet and rushed to my side. "Maybe you shouldn't sit up."

"Yes, lie down," Dad said.

Brad fluffed a pillow behind me.

Dad covered me with an afghan.

"All right, you two." I slapped them away. "I'm fine. What's wrong with you?"

"I want to take you away for a few days." Dad sat on the edge of the coffee table, his dark gaze locked on me. "You and your mother. The blown-up van was too much. You could have been inside."

"I don't think so." I glanced from him to Brad. "It's possible, but the driver of the truck had to know I'd seen him. He also knew I would send a text or make a call to the police. The chances of me waiting to do that until I was in the van were slim. Was anyone else hurt?"

Brad shook his head. "No, thank God. Some damage to other vehicles, but that's all."

"Good. I think the van explosion was a warning."

"One you should heed." Dad shook his head.

"I've always known I had a stubborn daughter, but you're far and above what I thought."

"Leave her alone, Joe." Mom handed me a bowl of soup. "She takes after you. You couldn't stop talking about your tussle at the gym the other day."

"Things are growing progressively more dangerous."

"They do that when your daughter is involved," Brad said. "I could take her back to the penthouse with me. Security is top notch."

"Not unless you've room for me," Mom said. "What will people think?"

I hid my grin while dipping a cracker into my soup. If she only knew how many times I've taken refuge at Brad's place. I glanced up and met his amused gaze.

"There's room for all three of you," he said.

"Great. We'll pack a few things and bring her over after she finishes her soup." Dad clapped his hands on his thighs.

"Don't I get a say in this?" I glanced from one to the other. "This is my home. I'm tired of jumping around."

"What if he blows this place up next?" Mom planted her fists on her hips. "I'm not leaving you alone. Your father won't leave either of us, so that means we'll all die. Want that on your conscience?"

Here goes the Mom guilt. "Fine. I'll gather a few things."

Seemingly satisfied, they filled bowls of their own, and we watched the local news while we ate. Chance of rain the rest of the week. A revival at the local Baptist church. A house fire.

"Turn that up." I set my bowl on the coffee table. "That's Alice Wells' house."

Flames reached for the sky, devouring every bit of the once grand plantation-style house. How horrifying to lose such a place. Thank goodness no one lived there.

The camera panned the crowd. I gasped at the sight of Valerie's pale face among the spectators. Her hair hung limp around her shoulders. Lines creased her face. The flames flickered in her eyes. A smudge of soot marred her cheek. Had she been hiding at her mother's all this time?

"I want to go." I sprang to my feet and swayed.

Brad reached out and kept me from falling. "You aren't going anywhere."

"I saw Valerie. If she's there, then Bill is too. They'll get away."

"This newscast might not be live," he said. "It could be half an hour ago, an hour. I'll call the station and let them know you spotted Valerie in the crowd."

I pointed at the TV. "It says live."

"Fine, but you're staying in the car." He helped me outside and into his Mercedes.

My parents slid in the back. Mom tapped me on the shoulder. "Here's your gun."

"What the heck?" I turned. "How did you know I carried one in my bag? Have you been snooping?"

"Of course, I have." She crossed her arms. "If you're going to carry one, you should at least remember your bag when going to face a potential criminal."

"I just want to keep an eye on her until the

police arrive." I could see the spot where the camera picked her up. She'd been standing half hidden under a magnolia tree not too far down the drive. Unless she got spooked, she might still be there.

Unfortunately, we couldn't get close enough to tell. Fire trucks blocked the entrance to the driveway.

"Go see if you can sneak around to that magnolia tree on the right." I gave Brad a shove. "I'll let McIlroy know where she is and that you're going to keep an eye on her."

"I'll go with you, son." Dad pushed open his door. "It's always best to have backup. Give me your gun, Trinity."

I handed it over. "Be careful, you two."

"Keep the doors locked." Brad gave me a quick kiss. "We won't be gone long."

I watched as the two men I loved melted into the shadows and circled the crowd watching the burning house. No one tried to stop them or gave a shout of alarm. I sent a quick text to McIlroy letting him know where we were. We might just get away—

"Isn't that the woman you're looking for?" Mom pointed out the windshield.

Sure enough, Valerie climbed into the driver's seat of a beat-up Chevy Malibu and drove away from the fire.

"Go after her."

"Shouldn't we wait for the men?" I slid into the driver's seat.

"There's no time. I'll call your father and let him know to find a ride home."

I turned the key in the ignition and sped off. Car chases were becoming a regular thing for me.

# Chapter Twenty

"Don't pass out while driving," Mom said. "We don't want to die in a fiery car crash."

Her phone rang. "Hello, Joe."

I could hear his shouting. "What in the name of Hades are you doing?"

"Following this Valerie woman."

"Who's driving?"

"Your daughter. Don't worry. If she shows signs of weakening, we'll switch places like you and I used to do."

"You will not switch places while still driving!"

"You guys used to do what?" I widened my eyes, staring at her in the rearview mirror.

"Back when we were young, dear." Mom waved a dismissive hand.

I returned my attention to the road in time to see Valerie pull onto Interstate 40. She didn't seem to be in a hurry, driving the speed limit. I wasn't worried about her recognizing Brad's car. Couldn't remember if she'd seen it before. I did pray nothing happened to it, though. The last time I drove his car, I was forced off the road and hit a tree.

A light rain started. I turned on the windshield wipers as my phone rang. I pressed the button on the steering wheel to answer. "Hey, Brad."

"Turn my car around right now and get back here."

"I'm sorry, but if I do that, we'll lose her. She doesn't seem to be in a hurry. McIlroy could catch up to us. If he does, then I'll come back."

"McIlroy is busy here." Frustration coated his words. "He ordered you back."

"Tell your man we don't work for the police." Mom tapped my shoulder, then resumed placating my father. We'd both have fires to put out when we returned home.

"You're in no condition to drive," Brad said.

"I'm all right." Other than a dull ache behind my right eye if I didn't move too fast, everything was good.

Valerie took the next exit ramp. I followed. "I should go and concentrate on my driving. Love you, bye." I hung up.

When he tried to call right back, I didn't answer. He'd know I was all right by Mom still speaking with my father.

"I think she gets the stubbornness from you," Dad said. "This is too dangerous."

"We aren't doing anything but driving, dear. We aren't even going over the speed limit. Are we?"

I shook my head. Valerie drove like an old lady.

"See, dear? We're perfectly safe."

"Brad said Trinity had better not wreck his car."

"I'll do my best." I glanced in the rearview mirror in time to see headlights looming. "Uh-oh."

"Uh-oh?" Dad's voice rose. "What's uh-oh?"

"The big truck is coming up fast behind us." Valerie must have seen the truck because she increased her speed. "Never mind. He's after Valerie." The truck sped around us. The driver didn't even glance our way. Good. We wouldn't have to stop because of the danger. Not yet, at least

"Joe, you're starting to sound like a broken record. How many times do I have to tell you all we're doing is following. We have no intention of getting out of the car. Do we?"

I shook my head. "Strictly observation."

My blood ran cold as the truck hit the rear end of the car Valerie drove. She fishtailed on the road but regained control. The next hit was much harder. I felt for her, having been in her position before.

"The truck is ramming the back of Valerie's car," Mom said. "Get the police over here. Now. No more wasting my time with complaints that won't change a thing."

"If you get yourself killed, Lou, I'll strangle you." Dad choked on his words.

"I love you, too. Talk to you later."

Another ram of the truck, and Valerie careened toward a grove of trees. The truck slowed, then sped up as she crashed into a fence post.

I pulled onto the shoulder. "Let the men know we've stopped and that I'm getting out to check on Valerie."

"You're making a liar out of me, dear. I said we'd stay in the car."

"She could be seriously hurt." I shoved open my door, wincing as the throbbing in my head increased. The time for a pill had come and gone, not that I could take one while driving. I slipped down the embankment, Mom right behind me.

"Valerie?" I peered through the shattered window, then tried to open the door. Too wrinkled up to open easily. The trunk had popped open, though. "Mom, see if there's a crowbar in the trunk. Something I can pry the door open with."

"Ta da!" She brandished a crowbar. "You get her out, and I'll call your father to let them know what's going on."

"I'll need your help." I stuck the bar in the door and leaned against it. Nothing happened. By now, Valerie's eyes had opened.

"What are you doing here?"

"Long story." I pushed harder, grunting. "Mom?"

"Coming." Together, we managed to pry the door open and pull Valerie out.

"I have a lot of questions," I said, "but they'll wait until we get you safely away from here."

Thankfully, she could walk on her own because I didn't have the strength to help her up the embankment, even with Mom's help.

Valerie climbed into the backseat, Mom taking the front passenger seat. "Don't look now, but we have company," Mom said.

The truck that had run Valerie off the road idled a few yards away. We'd have to pass him in order to keep going the right direction on the interstate. "Make sure your seatbelts are on. It's going to be a bumpy ride." I sent a silent apology to Brad and sent the Mercedes hurtling across the grassy median, barely missing a tree.

Mom gasped. Valerie shrieked. I kept driving, heading back the way we'd come. The truck followed.

"Tell Brad and Dad to find a way to get to the police station," I said. I had ditched Bill once by going there. It could work again.

Mom made the call, causing Dad to start yelling again. "Relax. We're on our way back and we have Valerie."

"You can't take me to the police." Valerie gripped the back of my seat. "He'll find me."

"Who will?" I asked.

"Prentiss." She practically spit his name.

I arched my brow, then relaxed as the movement pulled against my stitches. "Are you saying he's involved?"

"He's as dirty as they come. He and Knowles are cousins. When I dated Bill, I spotted him having lunch with the cop. They were having a deep conversation about how easy it had been to come into some money. That was right after you and I gathered the rest of my mother's jewelry."

"Why didn't you say something before now?" I pressed the accelerator.

"I needed proof."

"Did you find it?"

"I taped their conversation on my phone. So I cannot go to the police station. I've done my best to stay out of sight."

"Not very well," Mom said. "We saw you on

the news. Did you set fire to your mother's house?"

"No, but I was staying there. I'm pretty sure the fire was set to either kill me or flush me out."

It worked. "We'll go to the penthouse. It's the safest place I know." I pressed the call button on the steering wheel. "Call Brad."

"Have McIlroy meet us at the penthouse. Tell him not to bring Prentiss. I'll explain later." Right now, I had to get us there in one piece. Please don't start ramming Brad's car.

"Be safe, Trinity."

"I'm doing my best." I risked increasing our speed again. The jacked-up truck couldn't keep up with the luxury car.

Mom clapped me on the shoulder. "You're doing great."

I couldn't remember being more tired. It was all I could do to focus on my driving. But there was no way I'd let Mom take my place while we drove eighty miles an hour down an interstate.

Brad agreed to have only McIlroy at the penthouse. "Your father and I called a ride. We'll be waiting for you in the garage."

"Awesome. We left the truck in our dust." I grinned and took our exit. Ten minutes later, I pulled into the private parking garage and exited the car.

Brad pulled me into a hug. "How are you holding up?"

"I need to lie down, to be honest."

He scooped me into his arms. "Let's take care of that right now."

The others followed us to the elevator and up to

the penthouse floor. Mom headed to the kitchen to make coffee while Brad surrounded me with my fur babies on the sofa and explained that he'd asked Shar to bring them over.

"Is she here?"

He shook his head. "She's sulking because she missed out on another adventure."

I laughed. "Maybe she needs to move in with me." I sobered and turned to McIlroy who paced back and forth, knowing I'd fill him in when I was ready. "Valerie, tell the detective what you found out about Prentiss."

Valerie pulled her cell phone from her pocket. "You'll hear everything you need on here." She sagged into a chair.

"Do you need an ambulance?" He narrowed his eyes.

"No. Just rest. I haven't been sleeping well since…all this."

He nodded and pressed the play button on her phone. We remained silent as Bill and Prentiss discussed the necklace and tiara.

"Who could have taken it?" Prentiss asked.

"How the heck do I know? I'm positive Valerie doesn't have it. She's been like a pitbull trying to find those things."

"What about the woman you killed? Her son?"

"Maybe. They're in hiding. Can't find a single sign of them. We need those items so we can leave the country."

"I know that," Prentice said. "I'm not stupid. Who's the brains of this operation anyway?"

"You are." Bill sounded resigned. "I just want it

to be over."

"It will be. Find Irma's kid, and we find the missing items."

"That's the end of the conversation." Valerie released a pent-up breath. "I can't find Willy."

I started to tell her he was five floors below, but McIlroy gave a slight shake of his head. Right. We weren't completely sure how much we could trust this woman.

McIlroy took her phone with him, with orders for the rest of us to stay put and get some rest. "I'll let you know tomorrow what my next step will be with regard to Officer Prentiss."

I didn't envy him the task of apprehending a cop under his supervision. Prentiss had been assigned to Waterfall because of police brutality and found a whole other bucket of fish to dive into. Unless that was his plan all along. Come to Waterfall and meet up with his cousin, kill off a couple of old ladies, start a scam, take off with expensive jewelry. Quite the plan, actually. Too bad they wouldn't get away with it now.

Brad settled Mom and Dad in the guestroom while I made myself comfortable on the sofa. Valerie reclined in her chair, snoring within a few minutes. Brad gave me a tender kiss on my forehead. "It'll be over soon now that McIlroy knows of Prentiss's involvement."

I nodded. "Well, I have a feeling he won't go down quietly." I almost felt sorry for the dirty cop when McIlroy got a hold of him. Almost.

# Chapter Twenty-one

The next morning, I stretched, awakening every sore muscle and inch of bruised skin. Not as bad as the day before. I'd live. I sat up and smiled as Brad entered the room.

"Did you sleep all right? You should have taken the bed." He gave me a good-morning kiss that woke me up better than any coffee could.

"You're too tall for the sofa. I slept great." I glanced at the empty chair where Valerie had slept.

"She's in the shower."

"My parents?"

"In the kitchen. We decided to let you sleep in."

"Thank you all very much for that." I held out my hand for him to help me to my feet. "Is Mom making omelets?"

"Ham and cheese." With a gentle grip of my hand, he led me to the kitchen and settled me onto a chair as if I were an invalid. "I've a full day ahead of me at work. Can I trust you to behave and stay here?"

"I'll make sure both of these ladies stay put," Dad said. "We'll watch comedies all day like the idle rich."

I wasn't quite sure that was how the rich spent their days but didn't argue. In fact, I knew the rich spent their days working hard to get richer. At least the ones I'd met. Still, a day of relaxing sounded good. I only had one item on my to-do list and that was to speak once more with Willy and Sally to see if they knew anything more. Seeing Valerie might jog their memories a bit. "Movies sound good to me." I glanced up as Valerie joined us. "You might want to lay low here today. It's safer."

"I won't argue with that. I've nowhere to go anyway." She sat at the table, accepting a cup of coffee from my mother. "When this is over, I'm going on a long vacation to Europe. Maybe I'll move there. I can afford to with my inheritance." She set her cup down. "Maybe I shouldn't have gone looking for the missing pieces. It's completely disrupted my life and almost got me killed."

"Not only you." My mother glared from the stove. "My girl was almost blown up."

At Valerie's shocked face, Brad filled her in. "We think it was more of a warning than an attempt on her life."

"I think I owe you that twenty grand despite not finding the jewelry." Her features fell. "I didn't want anyone hurt. Wasn't my mother's death enough?" She shook her head, her hair falling forward and covering her face. "Why couldn't she let the scam go like any other old person would?"

Given the opportunity, Margie, Frank, or Hank

wouldn't have acted any differently. I felt better about Valerie, seeing how her mother's death did affect her. She wasn't as cold-hearted as I'd previously thought. I put my hand over hers. "Justice is almost done, and there's no need to pay me the rest of the money. I didn't find what you hired me to find."

She shoved her hair out of her face and smiled. "We'll discuss that later."

"Breakfast." Mom set a plate in front of both of us as the men took their seats.

Before Brad's bottom hit the chair, the doorbell rang. He excused himself, returning a minute later with Shar. "Our other invalid is here."

"The prodigal returns." Shar plopped into the seat vacated by Brad, leaving him to pull up another chair. "More adventure?"

Nodding, I told her about last night. "We're staying in today."

"Sounds good to me. So, Prentiss is dirty. I never did like that man."

Valerie glanced from me to Shar and back to me. "Why do the two of you get involved in chasing down killers? I mean, most civilians don't do that. They leave it up to the police."

"It started with the murder of a dear friend." I glanced at Brad.

"My father."

"He'd been murdered for pretty much the same reason as your mother. He found out something he shouldn't have. Brad and I didn't hit it off at first. I thought he wanted to raise my rent—"

"Which I fully intended to until I met the people

who would be harmed by that increase." He smiled. "So, I found other ways to recoup some of my father's losses. By renovating and building the theater."

"Brad was the primary suspect in his father's death, mainly because his father's cat hated the cologne he wore. The same cologne worn by the killer. Brad and I made a truce, he asked me to help him clear his name, and voilà."

"It's an addiction for her now." Brad laughed and bit into his omelet. "My gray hairs increase with every murder she gets involved in."

"What about you?" Valerie transferred her attention to Shar.

"For the pure adrenaline rush." She grinned. "I stepped into help right after I got hired and was hooked like a largemouth bass. That's why I get all butthurt when Trinity goes on an adventure without me. Escaping danger shows me that a fifty-year-old woman has a lot of life and fight left in her."

"Of course, you do." Mom handed her a plate. "I'm ten years older and not even close to too old for fun and adventure. Joe and I just returned from a long trip around Europe. We didn't run into any murders, but it was still a grand adventure."

Brad stood, setting his napkin next to his plate. "I need to run. I'll see you for supper tonight. We'll dine in." He kissed me and strolled from the penthouse.

"I want to visit Willy and Sally," I said the moment he was gone. "It'll be safe enough since they're only five floors down."

"You knew they were here?" Valerie's brows

rose to her hairline.

"I brought them here. McIlroy was too close to finding them. This place has the best security around."

"So much for movie day," Dad said. "Guess I'll work on the new house. Can't leave Honey and Prince alone for long if we want a house to return to."

"They're settling down," Mom said.

"At least you aren't leaving the building." Brad poked his head around the corner. "I knew there was something going on in that head of yours, so I only pretended to leave. Leaving for good now." He blew me a kiss and ducked out of sight.

"He can almost read my mind, that man." I smiled, only a little embarrassed at getting caught. "I'm beginning to like it."

"Finding a good man is like finding the other half of you," Mom said, patting my shoulder as she sat next to me. Always the last to eat, my mother. "Mind if I come along when you interrogate these young people? I've nothing else to do. Your father plans on painting the master bedroom at our new house, and the fumes always bother me."

"Sure." I smiled. "You can make sure I don't overdo things, being in such a frail physical state." I knew exactly why she wanted to come along and not work on her new home.

"Busted." She laughed.

After cleaning up the dishes and promising my father we'd respect Brad's wishes not to leave the building, we four women and Sheba exited the elevator on floor five while Dad continued down to the garage level. If Willy and Sally were working somewhere in the building, I'd ask the concierge to find them and send them up. Being Brad's girlfriend had more perks than just the pleasure of his company.

I knocked several times before a sleepy Willy answered the door. "Yeah? It's only eight. Too early to deal with you."

"Half the day's gone," I said, repeating one of my father's common expressions. "May we come in?"

He bowed and waved us forward, frowning at Sheba as she padded past. "Quite the motley crew." His eyes widened at the sight of Valerie. "I thought you skipped town."

"Thought you did." She arched a brow. "Seems the same man targeted us both."

"Your boyfriend." His lip curled.

"Former." She strode past him and sat on the sofa. "Nice place to hide out."

Sally shuffled from the bedroom. "You're the last person I expected to see alive."

"Sorry to disappoint." Valerie crossed her legs. "Mind if we all sit down and have a friendly conversation? After all, we have the same goals."

"Yeah? What are they?" Willy fell into an armchair.

"Justice for our murdered mothers."

He nodded, his face grave. "How to you expect us to do that?"

"Did you know Prentiss was a dirty cop?"

"No."

She shrugged. "Basically, right now, all we need

to do is wait for McIlroy to take over."

"Then why are you here?" He crossed his arms, Sally perching on the arm of his chair.

"In case you remember something that will help the detective. I doubt Prentiss is sitting at his desk waiting to be arrested," I said.

"I don't remember anything, and it's time for me to get ready for work." He rose to his feet. "Mr. Armstrong said Sally and I could keep our jobs when this is all over. Not the apartment, of course, but it's a good job that pays well. I don't want to mess that up."

"He won't fire you for talking to me." I wouldn't buy into that lame excuse. "In the past we've had to pull information from you inch by painful inch. We've got an empty day ahead of us, so here we are. Do you remember anything or not?"

His shoulders slumped, and he sat back down. "I've never met this Prentiss cop, but I did see Knowlson speaking to another man right before Sally and I ran to hide in your apartment. I heard the other man say there were two more that needed disposing of. That's all I needed in order to take my girl and run."

"Same as my story," Valerie mumbled.

Mom narrowed her eyes at Willy. "I know when someone is lying, young man."

"Fine." He leaped to his feet and rushed to the bedroom.

"Mom always could get me to vomit the truth." I shot her a loving look. "I appreciate that now."

Willy returned with a backpack which he dropped in Valerie's lap. "I lied about most of it.

They're after us because I broke into Knowlson's house and took these."

I leaned over as Valerie opened the pack. Sparkling up at us was a diamond-covered tiara. "How did you break in?"

"It isn't hard," Shar said. "I pick locks all the time for us, remember?"

Willy nodded. "Especially if you can climb trees, and people think leaving windows open on the second floor is safe."

"Why lie?"

"I thought I could sell them and pay off my mother's debts from the watch scam. She left nothing behind but bills and a house with a second mortgage. I'm sorry."

He didn't look sorry. More like obstinate, judging by his rigid body language. "Looks like I'll get my payment after all. Thanks for finally being honest." Yep, things were drawing to a close. Considering the battering my body took this time, I couldn't be happier.

Tears streamed down Valerie's face. "I now have everything that meant the most to my mother. Except for the house, of course. She can rest in peace now."

"Not until Knowlson and Prentiss are behind bars," I said, struggling to my feet. "We'll leave now so you can go to work. I wish you'd been upfront with us all along." I headed for the door as Valerie zipped up the backpack. I opened it and stumbled back as Prentiss entered, a gun aimed at my head.

He sneered. "Easy to get past the doorman when

you're a cop."

Valerie dropped the backpack with a thud.

# Chapter Twenty-two

Sheba made a move toward the dirty officer. His gun hand swung toward her. "Call off your dog or I'll shoot her."

"Sheba, here." I snapped my fingers, fear threatening to choke me. Hackles still raised, she obeyed, her dark eyes never leaving Prentiss. My dog would obey unless Prentiss attacked me. Then, she'd happily block a bullet meant for me.

"I didn't expect to find such a crowd," he said. "I came here for those two." He motioned to Willy and Sally. "Where are the jewels?"

"I don't have them." Willy put his arm around Sally.

Valerie used her foot to push the backpack under the sofa. "Where's Bill?"

"Waiting downstairs." Prentiss twisted his lips. "This is quite the dilemma."

"Not so much." Mom crossed her arms and glared. "You can simply leave and run off to Mexico, no one the wiser."

"Not without what I came for." He peered out the window. "Bill's going to have a coronary."

"One less moron for us to deal with," Shar sneered, sitting on the sofa and blocking the backpack with her legs. "What's your great plan now?" She shifted toward Sally. "Hush, girl. You're giving me a headache." She frowned at the sobbing girl. "If you shoot someone, shoot her first."

"What's the matter with you?" Mom went to console Sally.

I stifled a grin, knowing exactly what my friend was up to. While Sally's crying would become annoying after a while, that wasn't the reason for Shar's coldness. She created a distraction to keep Prentiss occupied while we came up with a plan.

"I can't abide spineless crybabies." Shar hitched her chin.

"That's no reason to be cruel in these circumstances."

Willy's head whipped from Shar to Mom and back to Shar so fast I thought he'd lose a screw, and his head would go rolling across the floor. His Adam's apple bobbed, his face pale. What did he think would happen if he went up against men like Prentiss and Knowlson? They'd eventually catch up to him.

While the others played their charade, I kept a calming hand on Sheba's head and peered out the window to see a van idling in front of the building. "How long will he sit out there?" I cut a glance at Prentiss.

"As long as it takes." His gaze hardened. "I knew you'd be trouble the minute I laid eyes on you."

"Read the newspapers, huh?" I shrugged. "What's your plan? McIlroy is looking for you."

"I'm pretty safe with a handful of hostages, I'd say." He glanced back to where Mom and Shar continued to argue. "Those two are going to drive me crazy."

"Welcome to my world."

"Shut up!" He turned back to the living room. "The next one who opens their mouth gets a bullet."

Sally clapped her hand over her mouth to stifle her sobs. Mom handed her a pillow. The young woman shoved it against her face. Much better at quieting her.

Prentiss pulled a cell phone from his pocket and pressed a number. "There's been a hang-up…more people here than just the two kids…no, I'm not bringing them all down. That'll tip off the doorman for sure…no, I haven't seen the jewelry. Find a way to get inside. We'll use the hostages to free ourselves." He cursed and hung up. "Everyone on the sofa where I can see you. Make it quick."

We crowded on the sofa, with me perched on one arm with Sheba on the floor next to me and Shar perched on the other one. Mom, Valerie, Willy, and Sally crowded on the seat between us.

Prentiss paced in front of us, muttering to himself. The stress of having his plan thwarted clearly rattled him.

Mom nudged me with her foot. "Now what?" she mouthed.

I shrugged. Clearly, we needed a plan, but I was coming up empty. I contemplated handing over the backpack, but once he had it, he'd have no reason to keep us alive. Still two deaths of two separate women were a lot different than killing six people at once. That became a mass murder, didn't it?

Occasionally, Prentiss would shoot us a furtive glance during his pacing. Then, he'd glance out the window, then back to us. His movements grew more frantic.

I recognized the danger in his escalating behavior and took the chance of getting to my feet.

Prentiss whirled, gun up. "What are you doing?"

Pointing toward the hallway, I took a step in that direction, mouthing, "bathroom."

"I guess so. It's not like you can climb out a window and jump five stories."

True. But I would take the opportunity to make a phone call. Inside, I locked the door and dialed Brad, including McIlroy in a three-way call. "I don't have long," I whispered. "Mom, Shar, Valerie, and I are being held hostage by Prentiss with Willy and Sally in their apartment. Outside the building, Knowlson is in a dark-colored van. He's trying to find a way in so he and Prentiss can figure out what to do with us."

Brad cleared his throat. "I'll contact the doorman not to stop him from coming in. It's best we know where both men are."

"Right," McIlroy said. "Don't antagonize either of them, Trinity. Cooperate, and we'll get all of you out safely."

Footsteps outside the door had me rushing to hang up. I took care of business and flushed. The footsteps receded. I slipped my cell phone back into my pocket and stepped into the hall.

Prentiss narrowed his eyes as I rejoined the others. "Took you long enough."

"I needed to compose myself. I'm a little stressed." I resumed my seat on the sofa, once again calming Sheba by putting my hand on her head. Tension rippled through her. One aggressive move from Prentiss and she'd attack.

A knock sounded at the door.

Sally shrieked.

The rest of us jerked.

"Answer it." Prentiss waved his gun at Willy.

Willy opened the door and let Knowlson in.

I ducked my head to hide my satisfaction. Taking the risk of calling Brad and the detective had worked. We were all in one place.

"Did you have any trouble?" Prentiss asked his partner.

"Nope. Waltzed right in and asked for Willy Grable. The doorman told me this apartment. Easy."

"Too easy." Prentiss's face darkened. "It's a trap. Everyone on their feet. Bill, get your gun out. It'll take both of us to corral this group down to the garage."

Bill glanced at Valerie. "Where's the jewelry?"

"I don't have it. I thought you did." It never amazed me at how well she could lie. My thoughts were always written across my face.

"Stay in a close group," Prentiss ordered. "Anyone who tries to run will be the first one shot."

"Where are we going to take them?" Bill yanked Valerie to her feet.

"Somewhere out of town. We'll lock them up

somewhere. Whatever happens after that is up to them. We'll be long gone."

"But the diamonds?"

"We'll make do with what we have." Prentiss opened the door. "Let's go, folks. We're all one big happy group going to lunch. Got it? Nod if you understand."

We nodded as one and crossed the hall to the elevator.

"Stay alert," I whispered.

Mom nodded. We might find a chance to escape in the garage. Cement pillars, dumpsters, lots of cars. All we'd need was a distraction. I hoped I could come up with one that didn't get me killed.

Since the elevator went straight to the garage level, no one saw our group emerge. It being a weekday, there weren't as many cars as I'd hoped. Most residents had day jobs, and those who worked in the building parked further away, leaving the spots closest to the elevator open for residents.

A dumpster sat to one side of the elevator, too close to provide the protection I sought. It became clear my plan had a lot of holes. "Where are we going?"

"The van parked over there," Bill said. "Leave the dog behind, or I shoot it. We don't have room."

"Stay, Sheba." My throat seized. I was leaving behind my best protector since I'd left my bag and gun in the penthouse. Things were unraveling at an alarming rate, and I feared we wouldn't escape. If they got us in the van, it would be over.

"She's fainting." I reached for Mom.

Catching my cue, my mother sighed, and her

legs buckled. She put the back of her hand to her forehead. "Oh, my heart."

"Leave her." Bill glanced at the van. "We're almost there."

"I can't leave my mother on the floor of a parking garage." I glowered.

"Someone will find her." His eyes widened as the gate to the garage entrance opened and a squad car sped in. "Let's go. Run or I'll shoot you. We have nothing to lose now."

Prentiss gripped Sally's arm and tossed her into the van. "Come on, or I'll drop you one at a time."

Willy climbed in after her.

Valerie glanced at me, clearly torn. Good. Her indecision would buy us a little more time.

"Stop!" McIlroy aimed his weapon over the door of his car. "This ends here. No one needs to get hurt."

"Try to stop us and I'll start killing hostages." Prentiss aimed his gun at Valerie.

I caught a glimpse of Brad skirting the squad car and circling the dumpster, moving behind Prentiss and McIlroy. I had to keep the villains from spotting him. "Help! My mother is having a heart attack."

"Good one," Mom whispered.

"Shh. You're dying."

Sheba licked my mother's face, her tail thumping the concrete. This could be the very thing that ruined my distraction.

"Gross. Make her stop." Mom shoved at the dog.

"She seems fine now," Prentiss said. "Let's go." He yanked me to my feet, using me as a shield between him and the detective. Slow step by slow step, we moved backward toward the van.

Knowlson spotted Brad and took aim.

McIlroy fired, catching the man in the shoulder.

Knowlson dropped.

Prentiss cursed and pushed me to my knees before racing for the van.

Hands shoved against him. He fell backward striking his head on the garage floor.

Willy slammed the van door.

Brad rushed forward and kicked the gun from Prentiss's hand. "Ready to give up now?"

The soon-to-be-former cop spit. "Someday, you people won't come out on top."

"Oh, I think they always will." McIlroy pulled the man to his feet and cuffed him, then turned to the rest of us. "Everyone all right?"

"Very." Valerie grinned. "We have my mother's missing jewelry pieces in a backpack in the young couple's apartment. These two men are going to jail. I'd say everything is grand."

"You do have them?" Bill's eyes widened.

"Yep. They were under Prentiss's eyes the whole time. Right there under the sofa." She marched up to Bill and slapped him. "That's for playing me. If I had a gun, I'd shoot you in your other shoulder."

"That's enough." McIlroy waved an arriving squad car forward. "Officer Rickson, take Knowlson. I want the pleasure of booking Prentiss." He took the cop by the arm and marched him to his waiting car.

Brad put his arm around my shoulder. "The fun

never stops."

"Nope." I leaned my head against his chest. "At least no one shot at me or chased me through the woods at night this time."

He laughed. "At least there's that."

"I, for one, can see why my daughter is infatuated with solving crime." Mom dusted off her pants. "I've never had such an adrenaline rush. Your father will be sad to have missed out."

"Oh, Lord, help me. It runs in the family." Brad's chest vibrated.

"Oh, yes. Things will only get more interesting from here." I smiled up at him. "You're a lucky man."

"That I am." He lowered his head and kissed me.

The End

Check out Four-Legged Suspect by scanning this QR code.

A beagle with a nose for digging up buried treasure.

Dear Reader,

If you enjoyed *Troublesome Twosome*, please leave a review on Amazon. Reviews are an author's lifeblood. Who do you think was the real Troublesome Twosome? Honey and Prince or Trinity and Shar? These characters are so much fun to write. I hope you've enjoyed spending time with them and are looking forward to the next adventure. Stay Tuned for the next book in the Tail Waggin' series.

Cynthia Hickey

Website at www.cynthiahickey.com

Multi-published and Amazon and ECPA Best-Selling author Cynthia Hickey has sold close to a million copies of her works since 2013. She has taught a Continuing Education class at the 2015 American Christian Fiction Writers conference, several small ACFW chapters and RWA chapters, and small writer retreats. She and her husband run the small press, Winged Publications, which includes some of the CBA's best well-known authors. She lives in Arizona and Arkansas, becoming a snowbird, with her husband and one dog. She has ten grandchildren who keep her busy and tell everyone they know that "Nana is a writer".

    Connect with me on FaceBook
Twitter
    Sign up for my newsletter and receive a free short story
    www.cynthiahickey.com

    Follow me on Amazon
And Bookbub
   Enjoy other books by Cynthia Hickey

### The Tail Waggin' Mysteries
Cat-Eyed Witness
The Dog Who Found a Body
Troublesome Twosome

### Tiny House Mysteries
No Small Caper

TROUBLESOME TWOSOME

Caper Goes Missing
Caper Finds a Clue
Caper's Dark Adventure
A Strange Game for Caper
Caper Steals Christmas
Caper Finds a Treasure

**A Hollywood Murder**
Killer Pose, book 1
Killer Snapshot, book 2
Shoot to Kill, book 3
Kodak Kill Shot, book 4
To Snap a Killer
Hollywood Murder Mysteries

**Shady Acres Mysteries**
Beware the Orchids, book 1
Path to Nowhere
Poison Foliage
Poinsettia Madness
Deadly Greenhouse Gases
Vine Entrapment

**Nosy Neighbor Series**
Anything For A Mystery, Book 1
A Killer Plot, Book 2
Skin Care Can Be Murder, Book 3
Death By Baking, Book 4
Jogging Is Bad For Your Health, Book 5
Poison Bubbles, Book 6
A Good Party Can Kill You, Book 7 (Final)
Nosy Neighbor collection

Christmas with Stormi Nelson

**The Summer Meadows Series**

Fudge-Laced Felonies, **Book 1**
Candy-Coated Secrets, **Book 2**
Chocolate-Covered Crime, **Book 3**
Maui Macadamia Madness, **Book 4**
All four novels in one collection

**The River Valley Mystery Series**
Deadly Neighbors, **Book 1**
Advance Notice, **Book 2**
The Librarian's Last Chapter, **Book 3**
All three novels in one collection

**Brothers Steele**
Sharp as Steele
Carved in Steele
Forged in Steele
Brothers Steele (All three in one)

**The Brothers of Copper Pass**
Wyatt's Warrant
Dirk's Defense
Stetson's Secret
Houston's Hope
Dallas's Dare
Seth's Sacrifice
Malcolm's Misunderstanding

**Fantasy**
**Fate of the Faes**
Shayna
Deema
Kasdeya

**Time Travel**
The Portal

## Wife for Hire – Private Investigators
Saving Sarah
Lesson for Lacey
Mission for Meghan
Long Way for Lainie
Aimed at Amy
Wife for Hire (all five in one)

## CLEAN BUT GRITTY Romantic Suspense

## Highland Springs

Murder Live
Say Bye to Mommy
To Breathe Again
Highland Springs Murders (all 3 in one)

## Colors of Evil Series

Shades of Crimson
Coral Shadows

## The Pretty Must Die Series

Ripped in Red, book 1
Pierced in Pink, book 2
Wounded in White, book 3
Worthy, The Complete Story

## **Lisa Paxton Mystery Series**

Eenie Meenie Miny Mo
Jack Be Nimble
Hickory Dickory Dock

CYNTHIA HICKEY

Secrets of Misty Hollow

Hearts of Courage
A Heart of Valor
The Game
Suspicious Minds
After the Storm
Local Betrayal

Overcoming Evil series
Mistaken Assassin
Captured Innocence
Mountain of Fear
Exposure at Sea
A Secret to Die for
Collision Course
Romantic Suspense of 5 books in 1

**INSPIRATIONAL**

**Historical cozy**
Hazel's Quest

**Historical Romances**
**Runaway Sue**
Taming the Sheriff
Sweet Apple Blossom
A Doctor's Agreement
A Lady Maid's Honor
A Touch of Sugar
Love Over Par
Heart of the Emerald
A Sketch of Gold

TROUBLESOME TWOSOME

Her Lonely Heart

**Finding Love the Harvey Girl Way**
Cooking With Love
Guiding With Love
Serving With Love
Warring With Love
All 4 in 1

A Wild Horse Pass Novel
They Call Her Mrs. Sheriff, book 1 (A Western Romance)

**Finding Love in Disaster**
The Rancher's Dilemma
The Teacher's Rescue
The Soldier's Redemption

**Woman of courage Series**

A Love For Delicious
Ruth's Redemption
Charity's Gold Rush
Mountain Redemption
Woman of Courage series (all four books)

**Short Story Westerns**
Desert Rose
Desert Lilly
Desert Belle
Desert Daisy
Flowers of the Desert 4 in 1

**Contemporary**

Romance in Paradise

## CYNTHIA HICKEY

Maui Magic
Sunset Kisses
Deep Sea Love
3 in 1

Finding a Way Home
Service of Love
Hillbilly Cinderella
Unraveling Love
I'd Rather Kiss My Horse

**Christmas**
Dear Jillian
Romancing the Fabulous Cooper Brothers
Handcarved Christmas
The Payback Bride
Curtain Calls and Christmas Wishes
Christmas Gold
A Christmas Stamp
Snowflake Kisses
Merry's Secret Santa
A Christmas Deception

**The Red Hat's Club (Contemporary novellas)**

Finally
Suddenly
Surprisingly
The Red Hat's Club 3 – in 1

Short Story

One Hour (A short story thriller)
Whisper Sweet Nothings (a Valentine short romance)

# TROUBLESOME TWOSOME